Common Ground

PAULA APPLEBY

ISBN 978-1-64003-933-9 (Paperback)
ISBN 978-1-64003-443-3 (Digital)

Covenant Books, Inc.
11661 Hwy 707
Murrells Inlet, SC 29576
www.covenantbooks.com

Sunday

I was waiting to be let in at the coffee shop. The first day of my summer job. By the end of the summer, I hoped to have at least three thousand in the bank. I also hoped to become a barista by the end of the summer, so next year, I could be a supervisor. My goal was to one day own my own coffee shop, serving homemade food. It would be good for the body and good for the soul.

I watched a man approach the dumpster. He looked around and then snuck into the dumpster through a small door in the back. Curious, I watched for him to come out. He came out through the same door with a bag in his hand, eating a cookie. The bag was stuffed with what looked like yesterday's throw away food from the coffee shop and a nearby restaurant. Our eyes met briefly, and I smiled . . . maybe sheepishly grinned. He was filthy, but he smiled back. He had a great smile. He waved as he walked off, eating his cookie. His coat was way too big and completely unnecessary for the already warm early summer morning.

The morning flew by. My head was buzzing with everything I had learned so far about how to make coffee; where the coffee beans came from; where the vanilla, mint, fruits and vegetables were grown for the flavorings and smoothies; how to make various snacks; and how to determine the "sell by" dates on our food. I had so much to learn, and it was only the beginning. In the fall, I would begin to learn the business side of working in and owning a coffee shop. One day, I hoped to be famous just like the little nymph on the side of my cup under my name, written in black marker.

I went out to breathe some fresh air and saw the same man from the dumpster earlier. Now, in the midday heat, he was lying in a shady doorway at the back of an adjacent store. Lying on his coat, his arm protecting his bag of goodies he had found earlier, he was sound asleep. Looking like an innocent child sleeping, he seemed to smile in his sleep.

"Hey, Bumpkin!" I heard a woman's voice call. The man sat up immediately and smiled at the woman, a disheveled plump woman, wearing a baseball cap and denim jumper with sneakers. He motioned for her to come sit next to him and opened his bag of goodies. Her eyes lit up, and her nearly toothless smile brought a grin to my face. They shared a "toast" with two bottles she pulled from a backpack she wore. Somehow, I doubted they really still held the expensive French sparkling water advertised on the label. Lost in their own world, they laughed and talked. I felt intrusive and looked away, guilty as I sipped my $5 iced coffee.

Back inside, I asked my boss about the disheveled couple.

"Oh, yeah, stay away from them! They're homeless, and they come around looking for free stuff. Don't let them use the bathroom. They like to use it to wash up and make a terrible mess."

"But it's a public restroom, how can we say no?" I asked in shock.

"Paying customers only, sweetie . . . You'll learn!" She pointed to a sign on the door. I looked at it then looked away, feeling bad. That would be hard to enforce, but I suppose she knew the rules.

Thursday

My fourth day of training, and every day, the disheveled couple had been around. Every day, I saw them on my break. Our eyes met, we smiled, but today I decided to say hi.

"Hi there! I'm Josie. What's your name?"

"Oh, aaahh . . . I'm Andrew," he said, taking a sip from his coffee cup with the nymph on the side.

"Nice to meet you, Andrew," I said and looked at his friend. She just smiled her nearly toothless grin.

"You work here?" He pointed to the coffee shop's back door.

"Yep, for the summer. I'm starting college in the fall," I said cheerily, trying to not sound too nervous and apprehensive. My boss had warned me he could be dangerous.

"Ah, lucky you! College! The door to the world will be open for you! Study hard, find a good job, and don't get into bad things. Life can be hard, ya know? Keep a good head."

I looked at the time. "I have to go, break is over . . . See you later!" And I got up to leave.

"Go get 'em, College Girl!" Andrew smiled and waved.

I wondered what he meant by "bad things." Drugs? Theft? Murder? Or just an unlucky soul who came upon hard times? As I closed the door, I heard the woman laugh and say, "Oh, Bumpkin . . . you make me laugh!"

My afternoon was busy. Making practice coffees, taking some tests on the computer about compliance issues, health code stuff, and learning some of our "recipes" for mixing certain smoothies and flavored coffees. I cleaned up the counters, took out the trash, tidied up the break room, and opened the back door to bring the trash to the dumpster. Two hours of daylight left. I wasn't afraid of going to the dumpster, but at night, I'm sure it could be spooky, especially if Andrew had many "friends" who hung out around it. I knew he would be by to scavenge, and I wanted to leave the bag of expired food outside the dumpster for him. But I also knew it was a violation of company policy. Giving expired food away or keeping it was considered stealing. It was a fireable offense. I shuddered thinking how awful it must be to have to scavenge a dumpster for food. I stalled a few more minutes and finally found a way to leave the bag near the top, easy to get to but still well inside the dumpster. Tomorrow, Andrew would not have to climb inside; he could just reach in and get it.

Friday

I wasn't scheduled to work today, but I decided to stop by and see if Andrew was around. It didn't seem right not to see him. He was already part of my day after just one week. I bought a coffee and stepped outside and around the side to the back of the building. He was there with his woman friend.

"Hello, Andrew!" I waved.

"Hello!" he said and offered me a cookie from his big bag of goodies.

"Oh, no thank you, I just ate a bagel, but very nice of you to offer."

"By the way, my name is Fred," he said and took a sip of his coffee.

"Oh, I thought you said . . ." then I realized the cup he held today said *Fred* in black marker above the nymph. It was my handwriting; I remembered writing it yesterday for the arrogant older man who insisted I remake his coffee because he thought I had put one extra sugar in it. *Fred*, I won't soon forget him.

I guess this was a game my friend played. He would be whoever was on his cup that day.

"Well, Fred, nice to meet you!"

"You met him yesterday, silly!" his toothless friend giggled.

"College Girl, you better get your head in the game!" And Fred laughed along with her.

I laughed too. What's the harm? "I guess you are right! I write names all day on these silly cups . . . I guess I just had too many in my mind, Fred!"

"Yeah, I mean they write your name on the cup to make it seem personal, like they *know* you . . . But honestly, you are not anyone to them. It's all just an illusion and how they make it seem okay to keep you coming back . . . You know?" Fred said as he raised his cup and examined the letters F. R. E. D.

"But we're all just faceless, nameless ends to the means, aren't we?" Fred said, looking into his bag of goodies again and plucking a cheese danish out.

"I suppose you are correct," I said.

It seemed sort of sad and a whole lot true to me, and somehow I felt a little queasy. And not just because I knew the cheese in the danish Fred was eating was probably really going to wreak havoc with his stomach after being out in the heat since last evening when I closed the coffee shop.

Suddenly, my vision of working in the coffee shop for the summer seemed cloudy. I had to make money. I had to pay for college. I had to go to college in order to get the job I would need or want. I didn't want to end up living on the streets like Fred or Andrew or his woman friend who had yet to identify herself. Could it be she was so lost she really did not know who she was anymore? Was she lost in a world of mental illness? Was this all a game to them?

My mind wandered.

They had done nothing to me. They were not dangerous. Just two people down on their luck.

"Go get 'em, College Girl! Show 'em what you've got!" Fred said and snapped me out of my dreamlike state.

"Yeah, it's my day off, I gotta run . . . See you tomorrow!"

I waved to Fred and his friend. They both waved back and smiled and went back to eating their danish and cookies.

They needed a good meal, I thought as I walked away.

Saturday

Weekends were extremely busy at the coffee shop. The downtown area was buzzing with activity. There was a plant sale at the town hall to benefit the ecology club from the high school, a car wash behind the school offices to benefit the sports teams in towns and just the general ebb and flow of lives going on. Shopping, banking, post office runs all the usual errands people did after a hectic week of the nine-to-five grind of the office. I got to the coffee shop extra early on Saturday to learn how to make some danish and put together some fruit cups. As I dished the fruit into the cups and added a dollop of yogurt to some, I thought of Andrew-Fred and how this little bit of fruit would give him some vitamin C and be a whole lot better for him than just the sweet treats he normally found in the dumpster. But I knew saving anything for him was against company policy. But nobody had said I couldn't buy him one or two. I'd look on lunch and see if he was around.

The morning was a blur. The line was out the door, and I ended up working through my morning break. By lunch time, all the fruit cups I had made were gone, and we were running low on everything. Saturdays were exhausting. And it upset me to realize we would not even have two fruit cups to buy and give to Andrew-Fred when I got done with my shift.

At lunch, I stepped out onto the sunny sidewalk and slipped around back. The doorways were all empty. Maybe the flurry of activity in the town scared them, or maybe they just didn't want to be seen by so many people. With only two hours left to work, I doubted I would see them today. Tomorrow was a beach day for me—finally a day to relax and get away. The money was going to be nice, but working full time left me very little time to see my friends.

Until then, coffee shop and little nymph on the cup. See you Monday!

Monday

The start of a new week and my first time working "the late shift" as it was called. The coffee shop was open until 7:00 p.m. most nights, but you were not allowed to work late and "close" until you knew the rules. My boss said I knew the rules well enough to close with Edward who had been one of the supervisors for over a year.

The shift ran well, it was not as busy during this shift until just after dinner. People coming home stopped to get coffee but nothing like the morning rush. I was cleaning the rest rooms when Andrew-Fred walked in and slipped into the men's room.

"I'm sorry, they are closed for cleaning, sir," I said. He turned and looked at me sheepishly and asked, "May I please just use the facilities?" I really didn't see it as a problem; it wasn't like he could make any bigger mess than anyone else just using the facilities. I moved aside and motioned for him to pass then waited outside.

Several minutes passed, and still he wasn't out. Edward came by on his way to the office with the deposit and saw me standing there with the mop.

"Everything okay?" he asked.

"Sure, sure. Just someone needed to use the facilities," I smiled and pointed to the locked men's room door.

"Not Dumpster Dave is it? He's not supposed to use the rest room. Sorry you didn't know . . . I'll remind him when he comes out."

"What's the harm? I mean, paying customer or not, it's not very dignifying to turn him away. And don't call him Dumpster Dave. That's just rude."

Gosh, I couldn't believe I was speaking to my supervisor in such a way! I knew the manager had told me the specific bathroom rules, and I'm sure there would be consequences if Edward told her. But I just couldn't believe this.

Just then, the men's room door opened, and Andrew-Fred came out. He looked sheepishly at Edward and said, "Pardon me and thank you. It means a lot." Edward put his head down and closed his eyes for a second. He motioned to the door and said, "We're closing now, could you kindly just head on out. I don't want any trouble."

"Bless you, Edward. Have a great night, College Girl!" he said as he passed by.

Tears in my eyes, I smiled at Edward and went into the ladies' room to start mopping the floor. I heard the bell jingle on the front door and knew Andrew-Fred had left, and the shop was now empty. Edward followed and locked the door.

TUESDAY

I walked into work with my stomach all in knots. Nervous about the way last night ended and wondering if Edward had left a note for the manager, I put on my apron, looked at our shift duty list, and got right to work.

By break time, I was ready for some time alone. Worrying and the constant morning rush had me pretty tense. I stepped outside and walked around to the back of the building.

"Good Morning!" I waved and was greeted by a big smile.

"How are you today?" I asked and sipped my $5 iced coffee.

The cup in his hand today read "Maria," and I wondered what he would say if I called him "Fred" today. I decided to just let it go. It was all just an illusion anyway. I decided to just call him "Friend."

"Fair to middle," he said.

His woman friend appeared from the other end of the alley and waved to me.

"Hello, Girlie!" I called to her. She giggled and sat on a bucket.

Just then I heard my name being called from the front. I said goodbye and walked back around front.

"Sorry to cut your break short," my manager said, "But they are short-handed at the other location on Elm Street. I have to run over there. Can I get you back inside a few minutes early?"

The rest of the week, she worked over at the second location, and I never heard anything about the rest room incident.

The summer flew by. I worked full time, and with my tip money and being diligent with saving, I had nearly double in my bank account than I had planned.

I had learned everything I had wanted to. I officially became a barista. I knew the regular customer's favorites, knew the recipes to make the baked goods, and understood the importance of "sell by" dates and how to order enough to make it through the week.

I was feeling really good by the end of the summer about school.

Monday

It was my last week at the coffee shop full time. From now on, I would just work when I had a long weekend and could come home to keep my name on the schedule. I had been having some great talks with Martin. That was his real name. Martin had been employed by a bank for many years. After graduating from college, he took a job in a local bank and moved up the ladder very quickly, becoming VP and bringing in a great salary. Things were great for him; he was married and had a gorgeous home in a wealthy suburb, a vacation home at the beach, and two nice cars. His wife was a pediatrician. She brought in a good salary too. They never had children, he said, which was almost unbearable for his wife to understand. She studied how to care for children, loved children, and devoted her life to saving them. Yet somehow they were never able to have their own.

"You never know what the bigger plan is in life for you. You think you know it all and then *bam* . . . life somehow derails, and you are left wondering where the next path is going to lead," he told me one day.

He also told me his wife decided to take her own life one night while he was at a dinner with coworkers. He came home and found her dead in their bathtub with a glass of wine and a bottle of medicine next to the bed.

Years of longing for her own child had driven her to the edge. Seeing the children every day and knowing she would never have one of her own, she just could not bear to live that sort of life.

He thought his life was over without her. He tried to keep things together, but without her, he saw no point to life. He became

15

belligerent at work, speaking in ways to customers nobody could ever imagine being spoken to. His appearance changed. The three piece suits he once owned became dirty, and he just never had time to get to the dry cleaners the way his wife had done for him. He just didn't care anymore.

Martin had lost everything. He couldn't understand why he and his wife had never had children.

"I suppose I could have been mad at God, but what's the point there? Without God, I would have had nothing, nothing at all. At least when my life derailed and the light at the end of the tunnel turned out to be another train coming at me, I knew with my faith in God all things were possible. There *had* to be a reason for what was happening to me. Living in the shelters, on the streets, with a friend or two along the way, I've always tried to keep that faith. It's kept me honest at least," he told me one day as I sat with him in the park.

I had been walking home after work and was surprised to find him there with a few other "street people" I had seen around town. He was playing jacks with the other men, and when he saw me, he waved and motioned me over. I met Bonkers, Green Leaf, and Lollipop. I introduced myself as "Josie," and they laughed at my real name. Lollipop was easy to figure out; he had a stick hanging out of the left side of his mouth. I assumed there was a lollipop at the end in his mouth.

"Is Josie your real name, or is it short for something?" Bonkers asked.

"Nope, just Josie. My mom named me after a college friend of hers, but *how* did you get the name Bonkers?" I asked.

"Oh you'll find out soon enough!" all three of them said in unison. I could hardly wait.

"Okay, then, how about you, Green Leaf?" I pointed at him.

"Aw, that's easy," Martin said. "He was a farmer back in the day. Farmed the big hills over to the west with his family until that drought came, and they lost all the crops. Never did regain their farm, but boy, oh boy, this guy can show you a thing or two about growing just about anything!"

Just then, I heard what sounded like a bird screeching behind me and looked back to see Bonkers hopping around flapping his arms and screeching. He was running around like a crazy person, hopping around, whooping and waving like a bird gone . . . *bonkers*! I got it!

"He just goes with whatever the mood is in him. See? He's *bonkers*, but in a fun way. Never does any harm, just one crazy dude."

So these three guys, Lollipop, Green Leaf, and Bonkers were Martin's friends. What a group. Somehow, it made me feel good to see that he had a circle of friends. And what a group they were!

Martin had been "homeless" for about five years now. His wife had been gone nearly three years before he really lost everything.

His once upper middle class lifestyle didn't exactly come crashing down, he said, it sort of just withered away bit by bit.

The bank fired him after a particularly loud argument with a customer, and he was proven to be drunk on the job. "I really wasn't drunk. They said I was. It was really just my mood was so out of control I needed to take prescriptions to control my temper, and they made me seem drunk. I didn't know myself most days," he said.

Without the job and his wife's income, the house at the beach had been foreclosed on months ago and then his home and cars were being taken as well. He tried to find a job, but weeks turned into months. Months turned into years, and soon he was living in shelters or on the streets.

Lost and alone, he just got by, he said.

"I never stole anything. I just took what was being thrown out," he said when I asked how he lived and ate.

"I just took things people put out for trash anywhere I could find them. I had the clothes on my back and my dignity. I did the best I could," he said.

"God kept me honest. Without that, you have nothing."

I had given him food all summer long. I knew it was against the rules to give it out, so I never really broke the rules; I just made it easy for him to find it in the dumpster. I never told him it was me, but I think he knew. It was hard to say goodbye. Harder for me, I think . . . Somehow he would get by, but for me, the unknown and I had to wonder—had I made him dependent on me? Was it now too easy for him? Had he gotten too used to me putting food out where he could get it easily? And after I left, who would continue that?

I worried.

But I had to go. College and my life waited. Doors would soon open, and I promised Martin I would make something of myself.

Monday Night

At home, I found an envelope on the table for me. It was from my Nana and Grandpa.

"For our college girl…with luck and love!" And inside was a $5 scratch ticket.

I took it to my room and snickered. Nana and Grandpa loved their scratch tickets. They sometimes hit it lucky and got a couple of hundred dollars, but honestly, I never got the point. If I had money, it stayed in my wallet or bank. I never wanted to waste it on "chances" like lottery tickets.

I scratched the little spots and thought I was seeing things.

$10,000.00 winner? Is that even possible? I looked again.

Yup. $10,000.00!

I put the ticket away in the envelope until the morning. I had to think about this.

Tuesday

I woke up feeling as if I had not slept at all. My mind raced all night. $10,000.00! First I needed to make sense of it. I took the ticket out and looked at it very closely. It was real. The amount was real. I had to call Nana and Grandpa. Then, I had to figure out what to do with the money!

I arrived at work feeling cloudy. My mind was racing. I just couldn't wrap my mind around the money I would receive when I turned in that ticket! My college education could be completely different from this point on. Could I bank it and not work next summer? Could I bank it and use it for the future?

Anyway, it was time to work. Four shifts left, and I wanted to leave on a high note. I needed to come back next summer and be a supervisor. I had a goal of owning a coffee shop one day and being my own boss!

"How may I help you?" I said to the first customer in line. I realized it was a woman who came in frequently and tested my knowledge as I stated what her usual order was. She beamed and said, "Yes! My dear, you have such a good memory. This place is lucky to have you!"

Just then my manager came by and put her arm around my shoulder.

"Well, College Girl is heading to the city next week to start classes. We sure are going to miss her!"

I found it odd she called me "College Girl" like Martin and his woman friend did. Had she heard my talks with them?

We talked about my upcoming semester and what my major would be and my hopes and dreams of owning my own business one day. It felt good to say it out loud. The woman wished me well and said she hoped I would come back on breaks. I assured her I would.

That night, I called Nana and Grandpa to let them know about my lucky lottery ticket. I thought Nana was going to jump through the phone when I told her. She started yelling to Grandpa and crying, and I could hear her blowing her nose. She was so excited. Nobody had ever won that on a lottery ticket in our family before.

"I just *knew* you would get something good. I could *feel it*, honey!" Grandpa said when Nana finally handed him the phone.

"What are you gonna do with all that money?!" he asked like an excited kid.

I told him I planned to bank it and keep it for later when I really needed it. I told him about my job this summer and how much I had earned and how I would not have to work during the semester except to come back now and then to keep my name on the schedule but that I could concentrate on school and not have to worry about finances. He was so happy for me, but the amount of money I had to spend for school was just so much to them. They were really excited to think the money from the ticket would help me in some way.

"And to think we only had to spend *five dollars* to get all that!" he kept saying over and over.

Later, as I lay in bed, I leafed through a journal I had kept of the summer at the coffee shop. I wanted to be sure I never forgot the early days; when I knew nothing about working in a coffee shop, how to make anything in a coffee shop, and how to have happy customers who want to come back. The quality of your product as well as the quality of your personality reflected back in the way people returned.

"Serve up quality, and you'll never lack for hearts around your table," that was a saying my Nana had engraved on a block of wood that sat in the middle of her kitchen table. I always liked that but never really understood until I was the one doing the serving.

I was going to miss the daily grind of the coffee shop. A funny saying we all used there—the daily grind—when we would talk about working there. I was going to miss the routine, the customers, my coworkers, and my new friends I had made in that funny little circle of homelessness that I had discovered. The five of them, completely different characters, coming from such varied lives and personalities, yet they lived almost like a family.

On the streets, they seemed to have a code. I never really could decipher it, not being there and really being a part of it, but I could see by watching them they had a code they lived by. I used to think it was rather primal, street living, but I realized it's not just survival of the fittest at all. They had friendships, they had love, and they had reasons behind it all. It wasn't just "mine" or "yours" in their world. They shared *everything*, and what struck me the most was that they had the least in life and gave the most. They never went a day without thinking of the others, sharing their food, their shelter, stories, and life. They didn't see each other as a group every day, but they always talked about each other.

Martin would always fill a bag of goodies and say, "My friends are gonna' think I struck it rich!"

I thought of all the times I sat there listening, sipping my $5 iced coffee and never once offered to buy him one. Was I embarrassed to go back in the shop? No, I don't think so. Was I afraid he would be insulted? Maybe. But what if I had?

"Martin, I owe you like a million iced coffees next summer . . ." I said out loud, putting my journal away and hoping I could sleep.

Somehow, these people had found common ground, and they had allowed me in. And I discovered I had common ground with them as well. Looking at it, I realized I had discovered a quality within myself that I liked: respect. Beyond the baggy coat, the disheveled look, the dirty hands and lack of superficial "things" was the people they all once were, still are, and would always continue to be—people with hearts and feelings and perspectives. And I realized, without even trying, I had learned to respect that.

That was our common ground.

September

It began with a lazy and long three-day weekend. I had moved into my new dorm; my roommate and I decided on a decorating theme over the summer, and the pink, grey, and black looked great, although several girls on the floor had the same color scheme. I had been a victim to subliminal suggestions: Pink and black . . . You know you like it. You know you want it. You must have it. I snickered at the ideas behind marketing.

So we were moved in and had three long days to discover the area that we would now call home with people we didn't know but somehow had to learn to depend on for friendship, help, sanity, and any other needs that may come up during the year.

We had to find common ground.

We took a taxi to the downtown area near the waterfront of the city. It was beyond beautiful. The sailboats were still very active on the water, joggers running along the paths, tourists out in full swing with cameras, families and lots of food. Oh my goodness, the vendors! It seemed on every corner, you could buy something to eat.

Yet everywhere I looked, I saw someone who was obviously homeless. My mind would wander back to the area behind the coffee shop, wondering what my little group of friends would be doing. Wondering if people were putting food out where it could easily be seen and retrieved. To my knowledge, nobody else cared enough to do what I had done. Again, I wondered if I had made it too easy, should I not have done it?

My roommate was looking at me; I was lost in thought as I watched a homeless man with one arm and one leg, trying to reach into a dumpster. I walked over, reached in, and took out a bag, hoping it was the one he had been eyeing. It was from an upscale, organic local grocer. It seemed someone had bought a precooked meal and perhaps forgotten it. It was still in the bag, sealed, and untouched. Along with it was a bag of chips and plasticware. The man's eyes lit up.

"You gonna eat that?" he said.

"Oh, gosh, no, I just wanted to help you reach it," I blushed.

"Well, gosh, there's an awful lot here, I can certainly share if you're hungry," he said, handing me the fork.

"Oh, no . . . really. I just ate on campus, I'm good, you enjoy!"

He hobbled off with a huge smile. Almost out of eyesight, he turned and waved, "Thank you, College Girl!"

My eyes filled with tears as I watched him continue on his way. I felt an arm around my shoulders and heard my roommate's voice in my ear, "Aw, sweetie, what a fantastic gesture! You are one amazing person."

"No, I'm not. He is. Imagine living on the *streets*, missing two limbs? Oh my goodness, how do you think he got that way?"

"Sweetie, don't worry your pretty face. Homeless are all over the city. You'll go mad trying to fix it all. Just know you did one little gesture. Like a ripple on a pond, it goes on and on. Just know you did good."

"A ripple in a pond . . . Yes, that's what I am. Now let's hope he carries it forth."

"Oh, he will . . . These down and out, homeless, and what have you. You know, those with the least to give always give the most. He's probably sharing it right now with another person. It's just the way of the streets."

We walked off in the direction the man had gone. I didn't see him again, but somehow I knew my roommate was right. I had seen it so many times over the summer.

Classes began the next day. The next few weeks were an absolute blur. With classes, learning the campus, meeting new people, figuring out dining times, laundry times, and homework times, I barely had time to breathe. I was so relieved to have a long weekend in early

October to go home and relax. I was loving school and the independence, but I was just homesick enough that I looked forward to a few days at home. I hoped I wouldn't sleep through it all and never get to enjoy my family and home.

LONG OCTOBER WEEKEND

I awoke that Friday to a cool breeze coming in the window and was glad I remembered to bring my fleece jacket with me. The first feel of fall, and we all knew winter would not be far behind. Everyone was shivering as we made our way around campus the last few hours before we would leave for three days. Stopping at the coffee shop, I got my first cup of hot coffee since last spring. I had been drinking iced coffee all summer and the first few weeks of school, but today a hot cup would be just enough to warm my insides with the cool breeze. I watched the trees blow in the breeze and noticed the fall colors coming, some leaves on the ground. Yup, winter would be here soon. I made a mental note to remember to pack my boots, scarf, and gloves for my return to campus Monday night. If this cool weather stayed and got colder, walking around campus would be uncomfortable to say the least without my early winter stuff.

On my way home, I got a phone call.

"Hey there, Josie! Say, we had a sick call for tomorrow, I knew you would be home and figured I'd give it a try. Want to work tomorrow? We all miss you, and I thought maybe a little extra money would be sounding good right about now?"

My boss sounded happy but also desperate. She must have called *everyone*, and I was her last chance. I had said I wouldn't be available until Thanksgiving break.

"Sure, no worry. I can work, just please not the early opening shift?" I rolled my eyes, knowing I desperately needed to sleep in.

"No problem there, I'll put you on the mid shift?" I could hear my manager shuffling papers on her desk.

"Great! See you at eleven!"

"You're the best, College Girl!"

It always made me stop and wonder. "College Girl" was something Martin had started. How did my manager know that nickname for me? Or was it just a coincidence?

SATURDAY

And boom! Right back into it like I never left! I was making coffee, handing out danish, and making fruit cups like nobody's business. Some of the regular customers were happy to see me back; I wished I could take time to chat with each of them, but it was crazy busy. The little kids junior soccer league were all in town for a tournament, and we had lines out the door with parents getting their coffee and snacks for the players and coaches using our Wi-Fi to check play times, field assignments, and the regular Saturday hubbub of the town. The morning was over, and lunch was almost done before I got any break. I dashed to the bathroom and ran right into Martin!

"College Girl! How are ya, sweetie?" He grinned.

"Oh, hey! How have you been? Gosh, it's good to see you!" I looked back where my manager's office was, nervous she may see him using the rest room and shoo him out.

"Oh, no worry, Ms. Gaines and I are good now. She lets me come in to use the rest room, but no washing up." He winked. "I just do my business, and it's cool."

Wow. I was surprised. Not a paying customer and using the rest room? Hmm. The rules must have changed.

"So I'm going to go sit outside for a few." I pointed to the back door, thinking he would follow me. I grabbed my jacket off a hook and pushed the door open.

"So my campus is so big. I just . . . Martin? Martin?"

He wasn't behind me. I stepped outside, and there he was, coming around the side of the building from the front. I guess he felt funny walking through the employee area and decided to go out the front like everyone else. I didn't say anything, just started talking again like he hadn't missed anything.

"So my campus is so big. I am finally feeling like its home, but it's taken me so long to figure out where everything that I need is. My room has a pretty view of the city, and I love to walk along the waterfront. It's so refreshing and peaceful."

"I'm so glad. I was thinking you'd get swallowed up by the big city and wondered if we'd ever see you again!"

I sipped my coffee. Martin fiddled with his jacket. It was like seeing an old friend but wondering if things had changed between you.

"Are you getting enough to eat?" I asked. I felt awkward, but I had been worried he wouldn't find stuff as easily.

"Oh, heck ya! Gosh, the dumpster here has never been so full and fresh. And someone left a flyer stuck on it about a week after you left about a new shelter that opened up on the other side of town. They serve meals twice a day and have a few cots you can stay overnight on if you get in early enough. I don't stay all that often. I figure I let the poor folks with kids who really need it stay there. I see a mother with two little boys there at meal time, and I know they've been sleeping in the car. It breaks my heart."

"But we have a new shelter in town? That's great! I mean, sad that we need it, but great that we have it for those who need it. But what will you do when it gets really cold and winter settles in?"

"Oh, don't you worry. I'll be okay. Been doing this a few years now. I have a place with my friends. We call it our vacation spot." Martin laughed.

He seemed happy and looked good. I had to get back inside and finish my shift but promised I would come say goodbye before I left for the night.

MONDAY

I made a quick trip uptown to visit Martin before I left for school Monday afternoon. I had ended up working Sunday half a day too, so we had quite a few chances to talk. Bonkers and Green Leaf had come by too. I never saw Lollipop that weekend. I asked about him, but nobody else had seen him either. They said he had been going home to visit family recently; it seemed they were trying to get him back to live with them, but he was having trouble adjusting to life within a house after being homeless for so long. Lollipop battled with addiction for years after having served in the Army, and that's what drove him to the streets. He had broken the addiction, but the stresses of military life, war and all that he had seen, lost, and been a part of ripped at his heart, mind, and soul. He had family who cared, and he cared about them. It was just impossible for him to live within the parameters and guidelines of life, he said. I was glad they had not given up on him and that he was open to their outstretched hands; it must be so hard to have that fog of a distorted reality within you. I said a silent prayer for Lollipop and hoped I would see him in November.

"Well, I gotta get back to school. I have a big test Wednesday and want to meet with my study group tonight. I'll see you in six weeks!"

Martin waved and said, "We'll have the turkey with all the dressing ready for ya, College Girl! Make us proud!"

I left before they saw the tears in my eyes. It was like saying goodbye to family every time I left this odd little circle of people.

Sunday Night

Settling in had been easier than I expected. My study group, friends and just general campus life had become like a family to me. This theme of family had been running in my head a lot lately. I had my family, and then I had sort of little "family units" all over. I had my work family and my odd little group of family from the streets along with now my college family, and each one had a specific role in my life.

We had all found common ground, and it was what bound us together.

Studying for our big test was so much easier with friends. Each of us had good input and asked questions I had never thought of, bringing a new perspective. We were all related majors and it made it fun to talk about how we could apply what we were learning to one day when we would have our own jobs, businesses, and lives.

My roommates Samantha and Kelsie were both hospitality majors. Samantha wanted to manage hotels while Kelsie wanted to manage restaurants. With me wanting to own my own coffee shop one day, we would spend hours talking about how one day we would all live together, work together, and have the perfect lives with Samantha managing some big hotel with a restaurant and coffee shop within it, managed or owned by us. We had each worked at the type of job we wanted to do for our career over the summer and had already formed some opinions of what we liked or didn't like about each one.

Samantha worked for a giant corporate hotel chain and had done training in another city at one point. She worked there for two summers and had opted into their management program early on.

Going to school was a way to get the proper accreditation she needed to be fully on board with their management program and get the title in four years. She would tell us stories about the exotic locations she could someday work for and it sounded like so much fun. Working for a giant corporation had its good and bad things. We would discover much of that through our long gab sessions over chips, dip, salsa, and coffee when we didn't have books to hit.

Kelsie worked for a local family-owned vegan restaurant at the beach. She and her family had been going to the beach every summer her entire life and knew the family who owned it very well. Kelsie would share stories about how fun it was to work for a small family owned business and the relaxed atmosphere that it brought, but also some of the struggles they discovered financially without the backing of a corporation behind them. Somehow it sounded ideal to me to have the family-owned aspect, the relaxed atmosphere and knowing exactly who was doing what without the umbrella of rules, regulations, and sort of being "owned" in another way.

My coffee shop, although being part of a giant corporate presentation, was a franchise and privately owned, but lived within corporate parameters. I was sort of in between the two styles of business ownership. While I liked the backing of the corporate world, often times it was tough to not have the freedom to do what our individual customers requested or our area and lifestyle asked for. Everything was like a giant box for us. We lived within it and it guided our every movement. Sometimes the box seemed too smothering.

I knew early on that I would always be grateful for what I learned at the local coffee shop, but owning my own business was going to be just that: one shop, one owner, one set of rules. And it was going to be all me.

And so life went on for us at school. We had papers due; we had presentations due. We had our disagreements over trivial issues, and we had our share of fun. All in all, college was proving to be everything I dreamed of and more. I was gaining knowledge and doing a whole lot of growing up.

None of us needed to work in order to support ourselves while on campus and all of us decided we needed something to do when we had free time. We began looking for something that would prove meaningful yet give us some luxury of not having to punch a clock and be accountable if our schedules got hectic. One day, while out in the city doing some shopping and having lunch, Samantha saw a notice for a local soup kitchen. It was very close to campus and was only open Thursday and Friday nights, Saturday morning, Saturday night, and Sunday afternoon.

"Hey guys, check this out. We could sign up to be volunteers there. We'd get a feel for food service but also make a difference and do something meaningful," she said, pointing to the notice. We took the phone number and website down and decided to do some research on it before we called. We'd look it up on the web and then take a walk over tomorrow.

Thursday Night

Having done our research, we all decided, along with a few other friends who were not busy and looking for something to do some weekends, to take a walk over and see if we could visit the soup kitchen while it was open.

We found it easily; it was along the waterfront but not in a tourist area. We walked down the side street, following our GPS directions and were surprised to see it was an old fishing shack. Decorated like a fishing shack, outside seating and the water behind it, it was beautiful! We were greeted at the door by a man dressed in khakis and wearing a polo shirt. He held a clipboard and asked, "Six for dinner?"

We were surprised! Is this a soup kitchen or a real restaurant? It seemed rather fancy to be a soup kitchen.

He could see the surprise and questions on our faces. "Guessing it's your first time here?" he grinned.

"Well, yes, we were looking for a place to do some volunteer work. We saw the flyer over in the grocery store near our campus," I said, speaking for all of us.

"Ah, well, yes, we can also use some extra hands, but understand this is not your average soup kitchen. We are Round the Table and have a little different philosophy. We don't give out free meals. We help those who need it and who are willing to learn to help themselves. Every meal here is $12.00, and you either pay or you work for your meal. You are more than welcome to come and sit at our table, but you will either pay $12.00 per meal or you will sign up for a work shift within forty-eight hours. There is always plenty do here at Round the Table. I'll give you a minute to think about that. Stroll the dock, see our herb garden out back, I'll just seat these folks and be back."

He motioned for a family of four to step in front of us. A mom and dad with two kids. The mom and kids sat at a table, the dad walked behind the counter, grabbed an apron, and came back out to another table and began setting it for dinner. Soon another woman came from the back with an apron and walked to the table where the mom and kids had sat and handed them menus, filled the kid's glasses with milk and greeted them with a "Hello! Tonight's special is PB and J. Who's up for that?" Two hands shot up and grins took over their faces. "Mmm . . . and fries, y'all?" the woman asked, nodding. Two heads bobbed excitedly. The mom glanced at the menu, put her reading glasses on her head and said, "I'll have the lasagna tonight, but only if Joe is in the kitchen!" Everyone laughed, and soon from behind we heard, "Would anyone else be making lasagna on the third Thursday of the month?!" The mom waved and laughed. "And I'll just have water with lemon, please."

We all stood with our mouths open, for sure. It was like a *real* restaurant. This was *not* like any soup kitchen we had ever been to. The man at the front door peeked over and smiled. "So what's it gonna be? You coming in or what?"

The six of us walked in and took our seats at a large round table in the back. There were fifteen tables with places set for eight at each table. Wow! There are 120 meals served each time!

"Good thing you got here early, guys. This place is *full* on Thursday nights with Joe's world-famous lasagna!" said the man who seated us. None of us could find much to say. We were absolutely astounded. We looked at the menus: Three entrees were listed along with two varieties of salad. Choice of beverages were water, milk, tea, or coffee. And then there were two desserts: pudding or cheesecake. This place was awesome, and we all wondered, *could you really get a meal like this for $12 at a local restaurant? How in the world did they do this?* We all watched silently as the dining room filled up. People came in and sat or went out back to work. Some came back with aprons and began either serving or busing tables, some began kitchen work. A few people walked past the window to the outdoor seats. Wow, we had not included those in our first estimate of how many meals were served! Six more tables out on the dock, each with four places to sit. Twenty-Four more meals! A few people worked out in the herb garden, cutting herbs for tonight's salads and dinners.

As we were eating our salads, two men came and asked if it was okay to sit with us. They took the last two seats at our table, which were also the last two seats in the dining room.

"Evening, I'm Peter, and this is Bob," said one man, reaching to shake our hands. We all introduced ourselves and made small talk about how we were college students.

"Pardon me, Bob, we forgot to wash our hands," and the two of them got up to head to the men's room. When they came back their drinks had been poured and their salads were waiting. Both men bowed their heads and closed their eyes. Their heads came up in unison as they said "amen" together. The six of us were well into our salads, having already ordered our entrees and each of us felt the blush of embarrassment as the men unfolded their hands and smiled at us. "Thanks to God for this place and for so many blessings," Bob said as he unfolded his napkin and placed it in the collar of his shirt.

"And thanks to God for our new friends and their ability to receive college educations. Education is everything in life. So what are you kids all studying?" Peter asked as he dug into his salad with his salad fork. We took turns around the table, talking about our majors and what we planned to do with our education. Peter and Bob marveled at our vision and clarity of what we all wanted to do.

"If I had been half as grown up as you, well, I may not be in the pickle I'm in today!" he said.

We never asked what his "pickle" was or what he had done for work. The time passed quickly as patrons came in, ate and left. We watched the line at the door grow. Feeling guilty for taking too much time, we decided we had better end the night and make room for more patrons. We passed on dessert, "Would you be able to give them to the children at the table in the corner? We really need to get back to study," we asked the server as she brought the dessert menu over for us to look at.

"Oh, I don't see why not!" she said and hurried out back to retrieve two boxes for the kids to take home some chocolate pudding.

Bob and Peter were ready to leave at about the same time as us and took money out of their pockets. They each placed $15 on the table and told our server to keep the extra as her tip. She blushed and said, "Very kind of you, but you know the rules. House gets the bonus!"

Bob and Peter explained to us that the staff was not allowed to keep the tips; it merely went to the business as a way of providing more for all. The staff was paid in meals and as a way to learn to work toward a goal, nothing more, and nothing less.

Between the six of us, we each had a twenty-dollar bill, so we left $120.00 on the table to pay for our dinners. That made a $48-profit from us toward the "house," and with $6 from Bob and Peter, our table had given enough to pay for all our meals plus $54-clear profit. We left, hoping it would help and having signed up to come and help during Saturday dinner shift.

We felt good yet oddly uptight at the same time. This place served *a lot* of folks tonight and, from what we could tell, barely scratched the surface of the needs in the city.

Saturday Dinner

We arrived about two hours before dinner started being served at 4:30 p.m. for a brief orientation. We learned about how to speak to the patrons as if they were just patrons at a restaurant. This was not a soup kitchen by the normal standards, it was a place of dignity and respect. As a server, you simply presented a menu, took their order and presented them with a leather booklet at the end of the meal. The menu was simple, consisting of three entrees, two kinds of soup or salad and two deserts. Children's options of PB and J, grilled cheese, or mac and cheese were always offered as well as gluten free options. The leather booklet contained a spot for cash and included cards to sign up for future work shifts if they were unable to pay. If we chose to not serve tables, we could bus them. This meant bringing drinks to them when they sat down, removing dishes in a timely manner and assisting them with anything they may need if their server was unable to respond. Kitchen work was also an option, meaning preparing the dishes to be brought out as the orders came in, washing dishes or cutting fresh vegetables as the salads required. The last option was garden work: picking fresh vegetables and herbs from the gardens out back to add to the salads as needed and watering as the sun set. On Sundays the garden work also included weeding.

We all chose our options and waited for the patrons to begin arriving. We were nervous at first, wondering who would arrive first. Would it be someone to work or someone to eat? Would it be awkward talking to people we had nothing in common with?

At 4:00 p.m., people started arriving. Some sat in the chairs on the docks watching the late afternoon water activity of boaters and jet skis. Others sat in the garden enjoying the cool shade and fantastic smell of earth, vegetables, and flowers. The children played in a small sand box under a large tree. By 4:30 p.m., the line was significant and the host started allowing folks in and recording how many were coming in.

I had decided to be a server and nervously took my first group of menus to the first table.

"Good evening," I said to a couple in their mid-sixties. They smiled at me and took their menus. They seemed more nervous than me!

"So, what looks good tonight?" I asked with my biggest smile I could muster.

"Anything!" the woman said. "We ain't had a home-cooked meal in forever! Thank God we learned of this place. With our last few dollars, we *figgered* we'd splurge and get a good meal. I'm think-ing that fancy chicken breast with carrots and mashed potato looks good!" She rubbed her belly and sipped her water.

"Mmm . . . just like you used to make, Ma," the man said and patted her hand.

"Oh, stop it. I'll make it again once we get back on our feet, you know that. I'll fatten you right up!"

"I'm thinking the big bowl of spaghetti and meatballs sounds good to me, does it come with garlic bread? I love garlic bread and parmesan cheese with my spaghetti," the man said with a twinkle in his eye.

"I'll check and let you know!" And I scurried off to the kitchen.

I asked the chef about the man's requests and was pleased he would get both his wishes. I then asked with concern that they said they were spending their last few dollars, that if I could tell them about the work situation.

"Sure, just keep it dignified, you know? Don't go and just blurt it out. When you bring them the bill just tell them they are always welcome to pay at Round the Table or they can come back to serve in any way they choose should they decide paying would put them on a tighter budget.

I went back to the table, feeling more relaxed than ever. What a great way to present it. The couple ate with gusto and had seconds on the garlic bread and mashed potatoes. When it came time to bring the bill, I handed the man the leather booklet and lingered for a few seconds as he opened it. He read the cards inside and glanced at his wife and then at me. He handed them to his wife. Pulling glasses out of her pocket, she scanned the cards. Her eyes filled with tears, and she mouthed, "Oh, goodness," as her hand covered her mouth.

"You mean we don't have to pay for this food?" he asked me.

"No, Sir. You just have to fill out the card and come back tomorrow or the next day for a work shift," I smiled at him and reached out to put my arm around his wife's shoulder. She sobbed softly and said, "We'll have money to get your medicine, dear."

I handed them a pen to fill out the cards and walked away. Wow, deciding between food and medicine. What a way to live. My worst decision that day had been cheese on my omelet or bacon as a side. I had some real awakening to do if I were going to work here regularly.

The rest of the night ran smoothly. We served over four hundred guests that night. It was exhausting, and as we all rallied to get the last dishes washed, the tables re-set for the next day, the floors mopped, and the bathrooms cleaned, it was just amazing to all of us to see the camaraderie between everyone. There were several people there working to pay for a meal, all of us college students, and a few who were the nonprofit agency workers. Until a few hours ago, none of us had ever met. We had virtually nothing in common, yet we had found some sort of common ground.

Common ground.

That term kept coming up in my life.

The beginning of the school year turned into the midsemester break and then Thanksgiving break. I was lucky to have my Wednesday morning classes canceled and could return home Tuesday night. I stopped by the coffee shop to say hi to a few friends and was excited to see I was on the schedule for both Friday and Saturday of the holiday weekend. I loved the downtown area on Thanksgiving weekend. We had our town parade, tree lighting, and other holiday festivities that took place, and the coffee shop was always the hub of activity with the big fire place going, serving hot coffee and hot chocolate and usually a school-age group would sing songs throughout the weekend to set the mood. It was so festive and fun. I went home happy I was going to be a part of it all.

Friday Afternoon

The day after Thanksgiving, and it seemed the holidays were already in full swing. The streets, stores and some homes began to have decorations and lights appear. There was a cold bite to the air, it almost felt like snow. Every year, I looked forward to the first snowstorm. I loved snow. I loved to watch it fall, loved to go snowshoeing and loved the look of the world in the wintry white. But this year, feeling that cold in my bones made me think of all the families I had been seeing at the soup kitchen in the city, Martin and his friends out back of the coffee shop, and just what it all meant to them. To us, it just meant turn the heat on, add a sweater, and crank the heat in the car. Around campus, I had big winter boots, a down parka and plenty of scarves, mittens and hats to wear when I needed to walk to class. If the weather was really bad, classes could be canceled, and I could just stay cuddled in my dorm, only venturing out to play if I felt like it.

But so many didn't have that option: their home was the streets, a shelter that was only available at night and limited to a certain number of beds. They didn't have a closet filled with warm clothes or a kitchen filled with food they could cook to warm up after being out in the snow.

And so the hustle and bustle of the onset of the holiday season began. Folks would come in for coffee, sit and talk, browse on their computers, do work and hang out for hours as the Wi-Fi allowed. Friday night brought the early kick off to the shopping season as the high school and middle school choral groups arrived to sing carols by the fireplace. It always drew a big crowd, and it was great to see everyone in a festive mood. I scanned the crowd during a slow time and was surprised to see Martin and his woman friend standing in the corner, just inside the door. She was singing merrily along with the carolers, and Martin was talking with a few men from the town. It was great to see them mingling and having a good time. I wondered if Martin knew these men from before, or if he just struck up a conversation with them.

All evening, shoppers came in to hear the carolers, sit by the fire, and enjoy some good times. We stayed open late with the shops, but the two extra hours of work flew by with everyone having a good time. Martin and his woman friend stayed until the end. It was so good to see them having such a good time, but I worried with it being so late where they would spend the night. I hated to think they stayed so late they would not be able to get a bed at the new shelter. It was very limited, and you had to be there right after the supper hour or you missed out.

"Hey Martin," I said as I collected trash from a table near where he was standing.

"College Girl! How are ya tonight? Goodness, what a great time this was, I'm so glad I got to come by!" His smile was genuine. The twinkle in his eyes led me to believe he was a true believer in the spirit of the holidays.

"Yeah, I'm home for Thanksgiving, but the time goes so quick," I said.

"Well, don't forget to come see us tomorrow, out at the old farm on the hill. We are having some turkey and all the fixin's and want you to be there!"

"I'd love to, but I have to work until three," I said, feeling a bit sad. Martin had told me about it the last time I saw him, and now I wasn't sure I could make it.

"Well, lucky for you, we are not planning to eat until around five or so. You'll have time to go home and get cleaned up and look real nice for our dinner. I'll tell Bonkers and Lollipop you are going to make it. They'll be so happy!"

"I'll see you then!" I smiled and waved at Martin.

"You too, Girlie!" I winked. She winked back and nodded.

SATURDAY MORNING

The quiet stillness of the morning on the way into work was refreshing. A cool, crisp feel to the air, the colors of the leaves on the trees, the sun just rising. I loved the early morning out here where I lived. I had gotten used to the city feel and the different times of day and all that they offered, but being out here in the country, our little town, was very special. It spoke to me. I couldn't wait to spend the evening at the farm that Martin mentioned. I loved being outside at this time of year, in nature, and smelling the smells. Although the farm had long since been an active farm, the smell of nature would still be there.

I had learned the farm once belonged to Lollipop's family, and he was allowed to stay in one of the old shacks on the land from time to time. Lollipop was having trouble getting back into life after his last tour of duty in the war and had become an addict after several trips to the hospital, rehab, and times with a therapist to control his terrors and depression. The things he had seen, lived through, and lost just somehow didn't seem to be able to leave him upon returning to civilian life. How could it? He had seen the unimaginable, lost countless friends and comrades, and seen lives taken just in the name of war. There were things he could never speak of that were locked in his mind and heart. He tried to speak of them with hours of therapy, but the only way for him to escape seemed through the bottle, drugs, and the imaginary world that was quickly overtaking his real world. It was a sad comment on how our soldiers returned home.

Lollipop was one of the lucky ones. As bad as things seemed for him and to the outsider looking in, he did have some good things in his life. He had family who cared and gave him the place on their land to stay, so he didn't have to live out on the streets where danger seemed to lurk in every inch of the streets, especially after dark. We lived in a small town, but the streets were the streets. Lollipop was able to stay in the shack, which he called his cabin, and he was provided for. Getting him to stay and take advantage of it was the problem. The demons that had come to live within his mind from that far away land and the evils that crept into his psyche in that land ate at him, and he was constantly trying to run away from it all. It pained me to hear him talk about things. It frightened me to hear the things he would say—unseen and unreal to me, but very, very real to him and not imaginary at all as it would seem to the stranger on the street coming upon him.

How I wished he could find the peace of the land, the beauty around him, and let it wash over him and calm him as the gentle rains did and begin anew as the long forgotten crops had done.

The farm would lend itself to a gathering spot tonight. I thought about it throughout the day. Turkey and fixin's Martin had said. I wondered just how would they get a turkey and fixin's set up there. And where would we all eat? I had only been by the farm one time that I could recall: during seventh grade when my class did an overnight camping trip. We rented some land from the family and pitched tents out on the fields where we spent the weekend learning about nature, cooking our food, and hiking the grounds. It was a team building exercise for us middle school students, but we had no idea we were learning from it all. We just knew it was amazing fun to be out on the hill at one in the morning watching shooting stars, the Milky Way, and the moon work their magic in the sky. And then to lie out at sunrise and watch the first light of day sliver its way across the sky. The smell of bacon cooking on an open flame and washing our dishes in the large tubs that were left along the farm lands from cattle long since gone. We loved every minute of it.

I hoped it would hold as much magic for me tonight as it did all those years ago.

Saturday at the coffee shop always went fast; today was no different. It seemed I had just gotten in, laid out the danish, and put the fruit cups together, then it was time for lunch. I stepped outside with my $5 iced coffee to the familiar area in the back of the coffee shop, but nobody was there. I figured Martin must have gone to the farm to help start the Thanksgiving dinner preparations. Three short hours later, I was leaving the coffee shop, saying goodbye to everyone as I knew I would be heading back early Sunday to settle back in for the final few weeks of my first semester. I was tired; it had been a long day, but I could not disappoint my friends and not show up for their Thanksgiving feast, whatever that would be! I drove home to change my clothes and pick up a jug of apple cider to bring with me. I got some fancy plastic cups to bring with the cider, not knowing what they would have out at the farm.

I found the farm with no difficulty. The old farmhouse had lights on. I hadn't realized any of Lollipop's family still lived there, but there they were, lights on in the back of the house, probably the kitchen and probably someone getting their supper ready. I drove down the dirt road to the back field, knowing the cabin Lollipop had referred to. It served as the infirmary when I had my school weekend there all those years ago. If a student was not feeling well, they brought them inside to this cabin to lie on a cot and get some time away. Camping and being outside for three days straight was a bit overwhelming to some kids who were not used to it. There were homesick kids, bug bites, odd rashes, sprained ankles and wrists: nothing a few minutes away from the other kids, an aspirin, or a couple of cookies and glass of juice couldn't fix.

I pulled up to the cabin and saw three heads inside one of the windows: Martin's, Green Leaf's and Girlie's. I wondered if Bonkers would be joining us and where Lollipop was. Just then Bonkers came around the side of the cabin, a large bouquet of wild flowers, ferns, and assorted branches in both hands. He opened the door and stepped inside. I could see him arranging the bouquets on the table and on a mantle above the fireplace in the old cabin.

They were going all out, I thought to myself. This was going to be some celebration! I sat in my car a few extra minutes, watching in silence as the scene inside unfolded. They wanted it to be perfect when I arrived.

I wanted to see the joy on their faces.

I got out of the car and shut the door. All four turned and looked out the window as I walked toward the front door. Martin flung the door open and shouted, "Happy Thanksgiving, College Girl! Welcome to our place!"

I stepped inside to a wonderful vision.

Thanksgiving sights, sounds, and smells! It was heavenly!

The cabin was delightfully warm, a fire in the fireplace and the table set for the six of us. There were pottery dishes and glasses on the table with a beautiful table cloth covering the table. A pumpkin sat in the center of the table with wildflowers around it. A woman's touch, for sure! I tried to hide my surprise, but it must have shown clearly on my face.

"You didn't know we have an interior decorator among us, did you, College Girl?" Martin said from the small kitchen off the main room of the cabin. My brain stumbled for a few seconds. Girlie? A woman's touch was always a welcome addition.

"Well, no, I did not," I smiled at her. It was lovely. Martin took my coat, silently hanging it over the back of a chair in the corner of the room, then lighting the candles that lined the mantle and sat around the room. With the warm glow of the fireplace and the candles, it was the homiest place I had ever seen. My brain took a few minutes to understand the complexity of it all: homeless and homey. It was an odd mix that thrilled my heart.

Just then, Green Leaf came in and began setting bowls on the table.

"Turkey's ready!" he announced. There was a large salad, baked potatoes and carrots, and then a turkey! A turkey! My mouth began to water. I wondered how they cooked a turkey in such stark surroundings.

Green Leaf set the turkey down and motioned to everyone to take a seat. I poured cider in each glass.

"I have to ask, *how* did you cook a turkey here?" I finally got the courage to ask as I filled the last glass.

"Oh, man! You won't believe it," Bonkers said. "This guy can cook *anything*!" he said, pointing to Green Leaf, who blushed outrageously.

"My family used to camp a lot, and I learned you can cook anything with an open fire. I just got this turkey down at the shelter and started it this morning out back in the fire pit. My family used to spend a lot of time up here, and the fire pit was our main source of cooking. We never had a real stove in this cabin, so we did it all on the open fire."

I was amazed. I never knew you could cook a turkey on an open fire! Green Leaf began slicing the turkey. It oozed drippings and circles of steam rose above it. Between the light from the fire, the candles and the smell of the turkey and fixin's, this was probably the closest I had ever come to a perfect Thanksgiving. My eyes filled with tears as we joined hands around the table.

Lollipop began to speak:

"Dear Lord, we thank you for these blessings given to us. This food, these friends, this shelter, and our full hearts. We are blessed in so many ways. Please continue to hold us in your hands as we partake in these portions. Amen."

The lump in my throat was quickly replaced with salad, turkey, potatoes, and carrots. The conversations around the table began with Lollipop explaining a bit more about his family and their time up here at the camp. It had begun as a camp for his grandparents, and over time some family began to build small houses on the land. His summers were filled with fun, family time as everyone gathered here. He explained the house I had seen driving in still belonged to his brother and sister in-law, and another sister had another house further up the road over the hill. They allowed him to stay in this cabin during the harsh winter months, and if the summers got too hot for him to live on the streets safely. His family was very involved with his life but had come to an understanding that he just could not live within the parameters of a house, the daily reality of what most of us considered living and fitting in with society. They supported his need for rehab from time to time and respected his need for letting it go and living alone. He lived in a strange world. My heart felt sad when he talked about it, yet I was happy to know his family always kept an eye on him.

"But enough about me, College Girl, what is it *you* plan to do in life?"

I explained my dream to one day own a coffee shop, serve home-made food, and be my own boss. I had decided early on, although internet coffee shops were the "thing," and everyone gathered in our town's coffee shop not just for the coffee, but for the free Wi-Fi, I would not have Wi-Fi in mine. Too many times I had seen people plugged in, focused on their own world, or communicating strictly via the world wide web and not realizing what was going on around them that I would not do that. My coffee shop was going to be good for the body and good for the soul.

"You mean have *real* conversations?" Bonkers laughed at me.

"Yes!" I exclaimed. The Internet and the connection had its place, but I want a coffee shop that has real meaning, where people can find common ground and make a different sort of connection.

"Well that sounds delightful," Girlie said. "I feel for the next generation. They will never know what it feels like to sit and talk and wait for something. They will never know the feeling of looking into someone's eyes across the table and really connecting."

"They will, they will, they just have to re-learn the art of finding common ground," I said.

"Well, we've all found it. It's not hard. You just have to listen to your heart. It always knows the way . . .," Girlie said, her voice trailing off, her eyes lost in the fire.

"Okay time for pie!" Green Leaf said. These pies come to us from Lollipop's family. When he told his sister he was hosting Thanksgiving here at the cabin, she made us a few pies. We have pecan, apple, and cherry. And I'll pour the coffee."

I just could not believe this. It was like pioneer times to me. This must be how they lived out on the prairie, in a little cabin with a warm fire and nothing but time to talk and just enjoy one another. *This* was the true meaning of Thanksgiving. When you know what you have and are thankful your heart is full.

And so were our tummies.

I offered to drive anyone back to town that needed a ride, albeit a bit sad thinking if I drove them back to town, it meant they would be sleeping on the streets, and thankfully they all declined. Green Leaf, Lollipop, and Bonkers were staying here at the cabin tonight, and Martin and Girlie said they would stay too, if they were welcome.

Their vacation spot! *This* is where they stayed when it got really cold! Realizing this made my heart full and warm.

They even insisted I take some leftovers home to my parents. I took two slices of pie and some of the delicious turkey and potatoes. I didn't want to take too much; I knew they would need something for lunch tomorrow out here at the cabin.

My weekend at home had come to an end, and soon I would return to the city and begin life as a student again. It seemed so foreign to me now—my life in the city and all that I would be doing with classes, friends, and roommates. I knew one thing for sure, with all that I had eaten this weekend, I sure would need a few good runs in the city to help get back into shape!

MONDAY AFTERNOON

Back into the swing of campus life, my friends were all heading to the river to enjoy the last few days of sunshine and warmth to study. We spread a blanket and opened our books and laptops and began to study and chatter about classes. As the sun began to set, we packed up and headed back to campus. After several hours along the river studying, we were hungry and decided to stop for a snack on the way home. We found ourselves at a popular Chinese food take out place. As we waited for our food, I glanced out the back door and saw the man I had seen my first week in the city near the dumpster. He struggled with his one arm and one leg to pull a box out of the dumpster. I wanted to run out and help him, but I figured he would probably be more embarrassed if I did that. I watched him pull himself up, pull the box out, and look in it. He then pushed himself out of the dumpster and put the box in a plastic bag he pulled from his pocket. He set the bag on the ground and pulled himself back into the dumpster, moving things around until he found what he wanted: a box full of crackers from the restaurant next door. It was probably expired and could not be used anymore, but for him, it was a treasure of snacks for the next few days. I watched him push himself out of the dumpster with his one arm and land on his one leg. He then hobbled along the alley between the buildings to the front of the restaurant and down the street.

Lost in thought, I hadn't heard my friends calling me, "Josie, Josie, Josie! Come on, let's go. Food is getting cold!"

We walked along the sidewalk, coming up to the man I had just seen in the dumpster. My roommate knew I recognized the man and would probably say something to him, maybe offer him some of our food and said, "Go ahead, I know you are going to."

As we caught up to the man, I coughed a small cough so as not to startle him as we came up behind him. He turned and smiled and said, "Your food smells good! Asian Gardens is one of my favorite places . . ."

"Oh, goodness, would you like some to take ho . . . along with you?" I asked.

"No, no, I just found some great treasures for myself, but thanks anyway. You need your food for study time, College Girl!"

College Girl? Did he recognize me from the last time? I wanted a chance to talk more with him, but we had to get back. We still had lots to do for class the next day and well, the food was getting cold.

Saturday Night

We found ourselves back at Round the Table for another night of volunteering. We were becoming very familiar with the routine and many of the patrons for the dinners. Every time I was there, my mind would wander, and I would think about how it would be to have a place like this for myself. I knew running a business of this sort was not something many would aspire to, the dollar called to so many, but for me, seeing the joy on the faces of the patrons who learned they didn't have to give up their last few dollars for a good meal or didn't have to make the choice between meals and medicine made all the difference to me. The children who came in really made it fun. They didn't know they weren't eating at a regular restaurant. They thought their parents were doing something really good by not taking them to the local burger joint, pizza place, or doughnut shop. They knew they were eating good food and learning about how vegetables grow, proper nutrition, and most importantly, they were learning kindness for others. They all thought their parents worked there, and they were just there for the night because their moms and dads were bringing them to work and hang out. It was like one big family.

Another family unit in my life.

More common ground.

I was realizing where the roots of my life would grow.

When I got out of work and was heading back to campus, I made a call to my grandparents.

"Hi Nana! How are you and Grandpa doing?" I hadn't talked with them since Thanksgiving, and I felt badly about that. They said they were doing well, the usual "old folks pains and whatnot," but on the whole they were doing great. They were getting ready to head to Florida after Christmas to visit some relatives and hopefully escape some of the winter snow. I was happy they would be able to be out of the winter weather but sad that I would not be able to see them much on my break.

"Why don't you come down to Florida for a long weekend or possibly a week?" Grandpa asked when it was his turn with the phone.

"Oh, I don't know, I have to work, you know, I don't work while I'm here at school, and I really need the money to make it through next semester. Besides, the plane tickets are pretty expensive, I'm sure." I said sadly.

"How about we give you the plane ticket for your Christmas gift, and you come for a long weekend? Five days? Thursday through Monday? We'd love to see you and spend some time with you, and the beaches there are just fabulous. I'm sure work and your parents will agree that you need a little break too?"

We agreed I would call and talk to my parents. It sure did sound good! Five days on the beach—time to relax in that warm Florida sun and eat some good seafood. I suppose it wouldn't hurt to let myself relax a bit. I missed my grandparents, and it would be good to have some good time with them.

Sunday Night

After calling to talk with my parents about going to Florida and getting it all settled, I then called the coffee shop back home to discuss the time off. Everyone agreed it would be great to have the time, relax, and refresh.

What's a girl to do? A gifted plane ticket. A place to stay. People who love me and want the best for me.

Florida, here I come second week of January!

It was a decision I would be ever so glad I made come the end of semester. The last few weeks of classes, finals, final papers, and assignments were torture. It seemed I never slept, spent more time at the library than my own dorm room, and ate more junk food on the fly than I had ever eaten in my life. There was very little time for outside activities. We barely got to serve at Round the Table, and the cold air had moved in with great gusto, causing us to limit our outside studying time. I missed our days along the river, walks along the city streets to shop and just sitting around campus enjoying the daily activities. The world became very monochromatic, stark, and cold. Christmas lights began going up and brought a certain brightness to the world, and the big red bows on the black light posts all over campus gave some cheer to the dreary world. But it was hard to stay positive and focused at times. As the cold nights turned to cold days and the sun seemed ineffective in warming our world, my mind turned to all the folks I had seen at the Saturday night dinners and of course to my friends back home. I knew they had the cabin to go and could get out of the cold, but so many didn't have the opportunity. I thought of the man I had seen in the city digging food out of the dumpster several times. I thought about him a lot and wondered how he got the way he was, missing his limbs and homeless.

One day, we heard music coming from the common quad on campus and walked over to see what was going on. The Air Force band had come to do a holiday concert with the ROTC members from campus. As the music played the crowd gathered, even people from outside the campus gathered to listen as it was right near a main road, and the holiday music filled the air. I scanned the crowd, amazed at how many had gathered to listen and sing. Behind a group of older men, I saw the man I had seen so many times digging in the city dumpster! He stood with his cane, singing beautifully, the voice of an angel could be heard high above the crowd. Behind him, I noticed one of the campus clubs had set up a table with hot cocoa and made my way over to get one. As I sipped the warm cocoa, I listened to the man singing. His voice was just so beautiful. Alto and rich, almost as warming as the liquid in my cup. Our eyes met briefly, and I smiled.

"Hey, College Girl, is this your campus?" he smiled back.

"Yup!" I reached to the table to pick up a cup of cocoa and offered it to him.

"Well, we certainly have no shortage of food every time we see each other, do we?" he laughed and took the cup.

He sang with the group during the next song, and I watched the crowd, listening to his rich voice. He saluted the ROTC members and waved to a few of the people in the crowd like he knew them. I was curious. Who was this man?

When the song finished, he looked at me and said, "Oh, my days of singing with the Air Force choir are well behind me, but I still get goose bumps thinking of those days!"

"Oh? You were in the Air Force?" I said with surprise.

"Sure was! Proudly served this country for two tours. It's how I lost my leg and my arm . . . but that's an ugly story. I won't share it on this beautiful night."

I began to realize he was a homeless vet just like Lollipop. He, too, had scars, demons, and ghosts of those days, his much more obvious from the first glance than Lollipop's and cut deep, I was sure.

We chatted a bit more about his days in the Air Force, and I learned he had been addicted after returning home, just like Lollipop. But his was not to shut the demons and ghosts down, he had come to terms with those. His addiction stemmed from pain medication and the inability to shut that down. Two different situations, but two very similar situations, really. In both cases, the drugs fed the needs they had after returning and fueled the desire to become mainstream in life after suffering horrific times that nobody here could ever understand. Each of them had seen loss of life, and each of them suffered loss themselves—one his mind, one his limbs.

These men were no longer whole, and no matter what building they put around themselves to call home, they lacked the ability to have that unity they needed.

Suddenly the holidays seemed dull to me. The stark, monochromatic world pulled at my heart, and the red bows on the black light posts just felt like the blood draining from my heart and soul as I thought about how sad things were for these men and so many others I had come to see far too regularly.

The Third Friday in December

The semester was finally over! I packed my suitcase and a few boxes of Christmas gifts I had bought to bring home and headed down the elevator one last time. I had grown to love my life on campus, but I truly needed this break. The next five weeks I could work and have no pressure of deadlines and the five days in Florida were truly going to be the best gift ever. I couldn't wait to get my toes in the sand and the sun on my face.

But first, I would venture out into the cold and wait for my dad to arrive and load my things in the car.

The first snow of the season began just as we turned onto the highway. It looked promising to have a white Christmas!

The Saturday before Christmas

The last weekend before Christmas, and the coffee shop was hopping! I stopped in to check my schedule and ended up working for three hours to help with the rush of shoppers and those just coming into the shop to warm up, hang out, and chat with friends and grab a coffee to help them get through the next few hours of shopping. It smelled even more delicious in there with the holiday scents and the fire going in the fire place. The crackling logs and festive decorations combined with the first snowfall of the season outside—it truly felt like Christmas.

A powdery six inches of snow had fallen overnight, and it was very cold. As soon as I got to the shop, I checked out back for evidence of Martin and his friends. Nobody was around. Good, I hoped it meant they were at the shelter or up at the cabin, having a good time together. As I came back in the back door, my boss greeted me, "Hey there, Josie! Looking for Martin?"

She knew his first name now? How odd to think just a few months ago, when I started working there, he was the dangerous homeless man not allowed to use the bathroom!

"Um, yeah, I guess . . ." My voice trailed off. I wondered how much she knew about my friendship with them.

"He hasn't been around much lately. I guess they've been staying at the shelter," she said.

I was relieved to know they were probably at the shelter but still wondered how she knew so much about them.

"Don't worry, hon. Your secrets are safe with me." She smiled. "I knew you were taking food out to them, and I sort of kept it up when you left. I never realized until you came along how homelessness can be. So many are thrown into lives they never imagined due to terrible circumstances. Lollipop's story is by far the saddest for me. My brother is a vet, and I thank God every day he has come back from his tours of sound mind and body . . ." Her voice trailed off.

I didn't know what to say or do, so I just stood there, blinking back tears.

"Thank you," I choked out.

"Aw, hon." She hugged me.

We went back to work and didn't talk about it again for the rest of the day.

Sunday Morning

I opened the shop on Sunday with Edward. I was happy to see he was still a supervisor since I had not worked with him in a very long time. The first thing I did was grab a shovel and head back outside to shovel another fresh four inches of snow off the sidewalk. Edward stayed inside getting the morning routine going. It was so cold with a bitter wind I was happy to see Edward had started the fire by the time I got in. I took a few minutes to warm my hands and face by the fire before joining him in the kitchen to get the food and coffee ready. It was still dark, but soon the sun would rise and the shoppers would be out in full force.

Someone had left the trash by the back door last night, probably as it started snowing they didn't want to head out in the cold, so I brought it out to the dumpster before we unlocked the door to let customers in.

From the door of the shop, I could see footprints all around the dumpster. My heart sank, thinking Martin and his friends had been by looking for food in the snow only to find nothing if our coworkers had not brought the trash out.

Just then I heard Martin's voice. "College Girl! Welcome home and happy holidays to you!"

"Oh, hey, Martin! How are you?" I waved and shivered.

"Oh, well, hey, tough to feel anything but happy when the world is all sparkly white and new again and the holiday spirit is in the air!"

"So true," I smiled at him. "You doing okay these days?" I asked, shivering in the cold wind.

"Oh, yeah, I'm getting by. We've been staying out at the ol' vacation spot a lot since winter is hitting early this year. Too cold to be out here, thankfully Lollipop's family is good about us all being out there."

"Oh, Martin, I'm so glad! You need anything?" I asked.

"I think I need for you to get back inside before you catch a cold. You look frozen! We're doing just fine. See you later!" He waved and started back out to the street.

The next week just flew by as every day at the coffee shop was straight out from open to close and with a few singing groups to provide holiday entertainment it was just one big party scene. Before I knew it, I was on a plane to Florida, and the holiday season had once again become a memory.

New Year's Eve had come and gone. Christmas had come and gone, and the snow continued to pile up. I was so looking forward to some time in the sun on a Florida beach with my Nana and Grandpa.

My second night in Florida, I was walking along the beach just before sunset and was watching a guy about my age play with his dog just at the water's edge. He would throw a stick out into the water; the dog would paddle out and grab it and paddle back in with the stick in his mouth, drop it at his master's feet, wag his tail, and shake himself dry. I sat in the sand for a bit watching the simplicity of a game of catch and wondered when had life become so complicated and messy? It seemed we were always on the go and always in touch with one another. I longed for the days my Nana and Grandpa talked about when they would gather with friends for drinks and a game of cards every Friday night. When they were first married and in the service, they depended on a close group of friends for their needs. It was like family to them when they were stationed places unknown to them. Nana used to say "my service family" when she talked about the men and women she found common ground with during these years. She would marvel at the fact that none of them knew each other and yet, their lives became so entwined that fifty years later, they were still gathering together when they could for mini reunions and sometimes larger reunions.

I was lost in thought over these wonderful stories my Nana had shared and didn't notice the guy's dog had run up the sand and was beside me with his stick. I felt it drop on my feet and was showered with his shaking himself dry.

"Harvey! No!" the guy yelled as he ran toward us.

"It's okay. I'll dry." I laughed and tried to get up and move away.

"Harvey! That is so not cool!" the guy was pointing at his dog and waving a finger. We both laughed, and I began to pat Harvey on the head.

"Really, it's not a big deal." I love dogs.

"Apologize to . . . to . . . Well, we don't know her name, do we, Harvey?" the guy smiled at me.

"Josie," I stuck out my hand to shake his.

"Brad," he said, shaking my hand. "And you've met Harvey!"

Harvey picked up his stick and turned his head so the stick hit me in the leg. I reached down and pulled the stick from his mouth and began to run down to the water's edge with it. Harvey ran after me. I threw the stick in the water and Harvey splashed in after it, swimming a bit to show off.

While Harvey swam around with the stick in his mouth, Brad and I made small talk. He, too, was here visiting his grandparents on his college break. They lived just two streets over from my grandparents in the same development, and he thought they played bridge together a few times with a neighborhood group. Brad seemed happy there would be someone his age to hang out with. I was happy too. He was easy on the eyes and seemed like a fun sort of guy. This trip could be really fun. We walked back to the development together just as the sun was setting. I had never seen sunsets quite as stunning as those on the Florida coast.

I said goodbye to Brad and Harvey and made a time to meet them tomorrow for a walk on the beach. It would be fun to have someone my age to hang out with, but I didn't want to not spend time with my grandparents. When I got back to the house, Nana had lemonade and cake waiting for me. It was a warm night, so we went to sit outside as the sun finished setting and the moon rose over the ocean.

"Nana, what do you think I should do? I want to own my own coffee shop, but I am learning the cost of having your own business is incredible. Between overhead for the building, insurance on the business, wages for the employees, and just the cost of running a business, I don't see how I can ever do it without being part of a corporation. I don't want to be part of that world. Working at the one I am with now has shown me what the corporate world can do to make things work, but it's also a slippery slope, sort of like selling your soul."

"Honey, you are far too young to have these worries yet. You have just started your college career and you may change your mind several different times before then. Just learn all you can, enjoy it all, and have faith that what you want in life will come if it is meant to be."

I did have faith. I had faith in my own abilities, and I had faith that what I wanted was good and would unfold somehow.

Tuesday Afternoon

After a morning of helping my grandparents with some errands and having a light lunch down on the docks, I made my way to the beach to meet Brad and Harvey. I saw Harvey running along the beach beside Brad with the stick in his mouth. He saw me and ran toward me, dropping the stick at my feet. I reached down to ruffle his fur on the top of his head and bent further to pick up the stick. I ran close to the water and threw the stick out. Harvey splashed into the water and swam out to the stick. With it in his mouth, he turned and swam along the shoreline a bit. Brad and I walked along with him in the sand.

We talked about the beautiful moon the night before and how it twinkled on the ocean. Brad studied astronomy and was very eager to talk about the moon and stars. It all seemed so magical to me and I was interested in learning much of the science behind it. I had never really cared for science in school, but to have someone who loved their subject talking, it was really quite captivating. After a while, he asked me what my plans were with college and after. I told him about my dream of owning a coffee shop one day. I also told him about the volunteer work my friends and I did at Round the Table.

"Why don't you combine the two?" he asked after I talked about how the soup kitchen worked.

"Combine the two? How would that work?"

"Well, you would still have overhead, but if you design it to work on the same principles as Round the Table, you wouldn't have the cost of wages. There would be a small core of regular workers, but the main staff would come from the patrons who came to eat and either pay or sign up to work, right? You would have the cost of food, but there has to be some nonprofit type of agency that would back you, I would think?"

"And my idea of not being a slave to the corporate world would add to that. At Round the Table, the idea is to sit, talk, meet, and be engaged with others. I will not have Wi-Fi connection. The idea will be to sit, talk, and learn about one another, perhaps help each other. I may just even have good old fashioned *books* and *newspapers* to read!"

"Why, Josie, I think you have *got this*!"

It sure gave me a lot to think about. The possibilities seemed endless now!

My week in the Florida sun went by all too quick. I had a lot of time to relax, sit, and think about the future and how my coffee shop would be designed, and I made time to meet Brad and Harvey every day for a walk. There was a spark between us, but we both knew it would be silly to start any kind of a relationship. Our focus was school and setting the right goals for our future. Brad didn't live that far away. Just a few hours on a train or bus, and we could be at each other's campus for a visit. We planned to meet up during spring break and maybe take a few day trips around each other's city.

It was amazing to me how comfortable the relationship was after just a short time. It was like we had known each other for a long, long time or were destined to meet.

Sunday Night

Back at campus, we all had our holiday stories to share. It was officially a new year, but our holiday decorations still hung in many of our dorm rooms. As we took them down and settled in for the second semester of the year, we shared stories. Everyone marveled at how tan and rested I looked and wondered why I had a silly grin on my face every time I talked about Florida.

"Your Grandparents must have some kind of spoiled you for *that* grin, Josie!" Samantha said.

"Well . . . I sorta met a guy . . ." My voice trailed off.

Just then my phone buzzed. It was Brad.

"And speak of the devil!" I put my finger to my lips to silence the giggles of my roommates as I talked with him.

When the call ended, they both came at me with wide grins. "Spill it!" they said as we boxed up the last of our holiday decorations and stored them in the closet.

I told them about Brad and, of course, Harvey and showed them a few pictures on my phone. After all the *oohs* and *aahs* about how cute he was, they said in unison, "So when is he coming to visit?"

I told them about our plans to visit during spring break. His was the week after mine, so it would work out great; we could each spend a couple of days seeing each other's campus and a snippet of our lives.

I told them about his love of astronomy and that he was studying forestry in school. Then I shared the idea he came up with about my coffee shop and how I could model it after Round the Table.

"Holy cow. He's not just really good looking. He is brilliant!" Samantha said. "I *love* that idea. It's like he *knows* you already, Josie!"

I had to admit, she was right. I had thought the same thing myself.

I also had thought sometimes common ground came when you least expected it. Nana was right. Just have faith, and if it's meant to be, it will happen.

Common ground. It tugged at my heart.

Spring Break Week

And just like that it was time for spring break. The winter had been challenging in many ways. We got snow nearly every week from early December right through until the week before spring break. Being on campus, we didn't have any excuse for not being at class, but oftentimes the morning classes were canceled due to the professors being unable to get in from where they lived outside the city. Having not been working the past few months, and using all my money for my trip to Florida, I was really looking forward to the time at home to just relax and have Brad visit for a few days. It was going to be so good to see him and really talk with him. Like most college kids, we did the usual FaceTime and Snapchat things, but being the old-fashioned girl that I was, I wrote him letters every week, telling him how my days had been, what I had done and what my plans were. The idea of sitting and writing my thoughts was not just romantic, but it gave me time to really think about what I had done and what I was doing. I also thought a handwritten note gave the other person time to really enjoy what you were telling them. It wasn't just a snippet of the day or a rushed few lines to let them know you were thinking of them; it showed effort, time, and purpose. And was I surprised when shortly after we both returned to our campus lives I opened my mailbox one day to find an envelope from him in it. He had bought and sent a card to let me know he missed me and was thinking of me! His notes and cards didn't come quite as often as mine were sent, but they came far more often than I ever imagined and it thrilled me.

Like Samantha said, "It's like he *knows* me," I kept hearing over and over in my head.

I worked the first two days of my break at the coffee shop. There had been some changes made while I was gone, and it took some time for my manager to go through the run down for me to be on board with the new practices. One of them was we now had an app for our chain. When you downloaded the app, your device was now decorated with a square featuring the little nymph that adorned the side of all our cups. When you opened the app, one of the choices was Coffee Cruise, meaning you could order while you were out, and when you cruised by the shop, it would be ready and waiting—no standing in line anymore. They were also now offering coupons and deals within the app to compete with all the other chains out there.

"Just one more way to make it more impersonal," I muttered as I meandered through the app pages on our tutorial.

"Now, Josie, you know this is a technology based world we live in, and coffee drinkers especially need things *now*." My manager laughed when she heard me and saw me roll my eyes.

"I know, I get it, my whole life at school is based on technology, and I get it's necessary to keep current. But I just sort of long for the old days when people went out for a cup of coffee to *talk*. Sit and *talk* and enjoy some time and space with others."

The whole world had become so disconnected, and although we were now more "connected" than ever, we were oddly so disconnected that I couldn't quite feel comfortable with it all.

My coffee shop would not be Wi-Fi enabled nor would it have order ahead, coupons, or reward cards. You would come in, order some coffee from a real person and read a book, sit by the fire or talk with people. What was so very wrong with human contact?

"Josie, hello? You are a million miles away. Finish reading here, so we can get to the practice part."

I finished reading the pages on the screen and headed out to the shop to play the practice part with my manager. As we were playing customer and clerk, my boss's boss appeared. Apparently he had been there for a while because he watched our interaction for a bit and then asked if he could speak with my manager and me in the back. My boss looked nervous as we walked to the back office. She glanced at me a few times and fiddled with her pen. The clicking of the point nearly drove me mad, so I reached over and took it from her. Placing it on the desk, I smiled. We had no reason to be nervous. I may be behind in learning this Coffee Cruise procedure, but we had good reason to be. I can't learn it from school.

"Josie, it is Josie, yes?" the big boss asked as he motioned for me to sit down next to the desk.

"Yes, my name is Josie." I smiled.

"Josie, I heard what you were saying about feeling our new programs make things impersonal, and I just wanted you to clarify that a bit with me. I want to know how you can think this is impersonal when we are giving the customers exactly what they want, when they want it."

"I . . . I . . . I don't mean we are not giving our customers *what* they want *when* they want it. I mean the whole idea of being connected to technology is what I find impersonal. I get that it's the way of the world and how we live today, but I just feel that we are more connected than ever before. Yet we are so oddly disconnected from the personal part of life. It just bothers me. Going out for a cup of coffee, a drink, a lunch, or dinner used to mean going out to spend time together with someone and enjoying the time together. It was time to talk, time to catch up, and a time to connect, reconnect, and unwind. I know we all need our coffee *now*. We are all on our way somewhere, and it's a "hurry up and get there" type of society we live in. But I . . . I . . . I just miss the simplicity of the slower times."

I realized I had talked a lot and said more than I probably should have. I watched as the big boss tapped his pencil on the desk over and over. First the point then the eraser, then back again. Over and over.

"This is a new program we feel will bring success and build our sales even more than we've had the past few months," he said.

"I hope you are on board with it and will give it a chance, we can't just dismiss every new idea that comes along just because we don't necessarily agree with it," he said.

"I never said I wasn't on board with it." I could feel my face turning red and my voice raising. Who was he to come at me like this? I merely made an observation to my boss in a friendly way. I looked to her for support but was met with her gazing at her shoes.

"If it is sales you want to build, then you for sure have the right idea," I said. I decided it was better to keep my answers short. Don't add too much and don't get overly emotional.

"Mr. Desmond, Josie is in school, learning the very aspect of marketing in the hopes of one day having her own coffee shop. She is a great asset to us and has worked during all her breaks and is actually one of my best employees. If it wasn't for her being in school, I would make her a full time supervisor. I'm not sure where this notion is coming from. I think she simply was pondering some ideas she has for her own coffee shop one day. I think you may be coming at her a bit unfairly," my boss said. I could hear her voice quiver as she spoke. She was clearly nervous and perplexed about this as well.

"I just want to be sure we are all on board with this. It's a very important step to our sales building push for the coming year. It's very exciting and opens a whole new realm of customer satisfaction."

I wanted so bad to speak up but felt it was best to just keep my mouth shut. I wanted to scream "It's not always about the dollar!" but decided this was not the time, place, or person to voice my ideas or frustrations to.

"I just want to be sure we are not turning this place into some sort of hippie hang out and refuge for homeless vagrants and other disruptive types," Mr. Desmond said, staring into my eyes for a reaction.

And he got one.

"Excuse me? *What* does that mean exactly?" I stood up and faced him full on. I would not sit and be talked to like this.

"I work at a soup kitchen at school, and I am involved with some homeless people whom I have become friends with. But I have never had them hanging out in this coffee shop like a "hippie hang out," and they surely are *not* vagrants or disruptive, Mr. Desmond."

My voice, hands, and legs were all shaking at this point. If I wasn't so mad, I would have fallen down, but I kept on.

"The place I *volunteer* in is a nonprofit soup kitchen with a wonderful and respectful way of serving the community and people who happen to be down on their luck. We serve all who come, and they, in turn, serve and return the graces they have learned. While at

Round the Table, patrons eat with others in a dignified way. It is *this* sort of business I hope to model my own after one day. I have enjoyed working here and learning all I can about how to run a business, how to produce a great product, and how to be the best boss I can be while filling a need I will find one day. I have *never* taken advantage of you, your business, or my coworkers, and I will not allow you to take my compassion and turn it into something ugly and shameful."

I sat back in the chair before my legs gave out. I could feel the heat rising through my face and head; my head began to throb. I just could *not* believe this is what he called me in for. One little comment, and he dug all this out of it?

"Josie, is it not true that you have been sneaking food out to the dumpster to feed the homeless who gather there at night?"

"That is not true, sir, not at all. I admit, I have been putting *trash* and food that we are throwing away where it may be easier for them to get, but I have never once taken anything considered good and still within date code and sent it out to them. And yes, I have allowed them to use the rest room, but they have always come in and bought something and stayed to warm up by the fire for a bit. I treat everyone with dignity, the same dignity I expect in life. It's not just a free hippie hang out as you call it. I resent that."

Wow. This spring break was *not* going as I planned at all. Here I thought I would have a great week and work, make some money, see Brad, and enjoy some time to relax; but this may prove to be the worst week ever. I feared I would lose my job any second.

My boss looked nearly as angry as I felt.

"Mr. Desmond, where is this coming from? Josie just got back into town last night. She hasn't even been here since Christmas break. Why are you coming at her this way?"

"I've received a few e-mail notifications from an anonymous source." Mr. Desmond looked angry. I tried to rationalize it. Was he angry because of what he *thought* I had been doing? Was he angry because I spoke up and refused to be belittled by him? Or was he angry because he had been duped, and someone obviously had it out for me and wanted me fired and went about it in the worst way?

We all just sat there, looking at one another for a few minutes. Mr. Desmond seemed to be reviewing all that I had said over in his head and was trying to form an opinion or come to a conclusion. He had backed me into a corner, and I came back with some real answers and clearly not the ones he expected to hear.

"Why do you work here, Josie? What is your goal in all this?" he asked me calmly.

"May I speak honestly?" I answered calmly.

"Of course, it seems we all may have something to learn here," he said.

I took a deep breath and began to explain my goal in life for my own coffee shop one day. I explained I never meant any disrespect and that I truly enjoyed learning how to become a barista, the business end of it, and the connected feeling I had to the community and my coworkers. I did add I was horribly offended that someone chose to report me in such an ugly way for doing something that may be against corporate rules when viewed one way but when it became trash and was taken outside it became anyone's property. If by making it easier I was breaking corporate rules then I would stop doing it, but I honestly believed in what I was saying and doing. I also explained that while I understood business was business, I had been doing exploring within the business world and had come to the realization that becoming a nonprofit was my idea of a business for my own business. Through my volunteer time and getting to know the circumstances behind this small group of people from my own town as well as the few I saw on a regular basis at Round the Table in the city, I began to realize there was a greater reason for opening a business. Making money and adding to the corporate greed just didn't work with what I had going on within my head and heart. A sense of belonging and being connected was what I hoped to achieve.

"And tell me about your comment regarding being more and more disconnected?" Mr. Desmond asked. At this point he actually took out a notebook and began making notes with the pencil he had been tap . . . tap . . . tapping earlier. Now, as he listened to me speak, the pencil no longer tap, tap, tapped on the desk; it rested on the corner of his mouth. He would jot things down in his notebook as I spoke and then go back to rest the eraser end on the corner of his mouth.

"I just feel while it is necessary and the way we live today, we need a break now and then. I hope one day to have a coffee shop filled with people talking, relaxing, and getting to know one another. You don't know another person's struggles or triumphs unless you have time to talk. You don't know another person's life sequence unless you talk. And you have no common ground when you simply dash in, open an app, and leave with your purchase. You have to *want* to be engaged with people. You have to connect. My idea is no Wi-Fi. I would have a fireplace and books, newspapers, and maybe a place for children to play. I hope to model it after Round the Table's practice: Everything is a set price and the patrons either pay or sign up to come back and work. Everyone is equal; there is dignity and genuine respect and caring. I know it's not going to make me rich, but I don't need to be rich with stuff. I prefer to be rich with stories, life, and what makes us who we are."

I realized I had talked a long time. I stopped abruptly and asked, "Am I being fired?"

I heard my manager gasp. It was like she had been holding her breath the entire time I spoke, and I had asked the exact same question she had been wondering.

"Of course not. I realize I have been misled. You are a wonderful visionary, and I truly hope your plan comes to fruition. It's a brave place to be in at your age, willing to enter life knowing you will never have much in the bank, yet you see yourself as richer than most."

I couldn't decide if Mr. Desmond was mocking me or acknowledging what I believed in.

"One last thing," I said before he got up to leave.

"And that is?" he opened to a new page in his notebook.

"I think it would be great to have one day a week Wi-Fi free just to see how it goes and invite families in one night a week for children's story hour by the fireplace. I know it's not going to happen, but watching all the families have their fun during the holiday nights here, it just sort of came to me."

"We can talk about that," Mr. Desmond smiled.

Mocking? Accepting? I still wasn't sure.

WEDNESDAY

· ·

Having been off the day before, I got to work for the midshift and was surprised when I got in to see Edward and the manager at the registers.

"Where's Rebecca?" I asked as I tied my apron around my waist.

"Um, she no longer works here," Edward said.

My eyes widened and he nodded. We silently spoke a secret language. It said so much.

Later on my break, after a few others had come in to work and the shop was slowing down after the lunch rush, Edward told me more about Rebecca. Apparently she was the one who had been e-mailing Mr. Desmond about me and filling his head with all sorts of lies. I didn't need to know any more. Someone like that had no place in my life. I had never liked her, but I tried to be fair and nice to her, knowing we worked together. But now that I knew she was gone and why, I didn't need to put any more thought into it. I believed in karma. Her turn would come.

Wednesday Afternoon

···

After the longest, most horrible day at the coffee shop, I had a wonderful night to look forward to. Brad and Harvey had arrived in town while I was at work, and they were waiting to take a long walk with me. We walked around town for a bit, and as we rounded the corner, we bumped right into Martin!

"College Girl! How are ya?" Martin grinned and reached out to shake Brad's hand. "You must be Brad!"

"I am Brad, indeed!" He smiled at Martin and shook his hand.

"Wait a second, how did you know his name? I haven't been here since the holidays!" I laughed out loud, knowing full well my manager had a few more surprises up her sleeve than she was willing to reveal right now.

Martin and Brad began to chat about the recent football game, and Harvey sniffed around a trash bin. He had found something good to eat and wasn't letting it go. "Like a dog with a bone?" Martin laughed and pointed at Harvey

Martin asked if we would be free for a game of cards and some snacks later. The group was getting together at the cabin tonight, and with us being in town, it just seemed right for us to be there. We decided on a time to meet and headed home to have dinner with my family.

"I didn't even ask, are you okay with that? Going out to the cabin tonight?" I apologized to Brad after we walked away. I hadn't even thought he may want to sit around at home and get to know my family or go out somewhere just the two of us.

"Oh, sure! Gosh, Martin is fascinating. He's led an amazing life, before and after his career, marriage, and all that. I'm looking forward to meeting the rest of these folks!"

Walking into my house and smelling the pot roast my mother had cooking and the warmth of the house was just fabulous. It was very chilly out and this winter meal was just perfect for my first introduction to my family for Brad and, of course, Harvey! His nose was in the air sniffing and sniffing like a hound! He made himself at home right in front of the oven on the throw rug. Nothing was getting by him! Curling up and snoring, we knew he would not be leaving that spot until dinner was served, and in his dreams he was first in line!

7:00 P.M., WEDNESDAY NIGHT

We pulled into the old farm and saw the lights on in the cabin. Heads were appearing in the windows, and I could see them all getting things ready. It was so fun to think of them working together to plan these nights, and having me as their guest must make them feel very proud to show off all that they had. In life, it wasn't much, but to them, it was everything. And that made my heart nearly burst with pride, knowing how dear they all were.

Once inside the warmth of the fire, the glow of the simple lights and candles they used and the smell of freshly popped popcorn made me sleepy. I sat on the couch, Brad sat next to me, and they began to bring more snacks over. Green Leaf moved the big table from the kitchen into the living room area, so we could sit by the fire and play cards. Bonkers was running around in sort of a crazy mood. He said it was post-holiday blues, but it seemed more like a little kid excited to be staying up late for a party to me.

"Hey there, Girlie!" I smiled as another bowl of popcorn was placed on the table.

"Hey there, Josie," she smiled back. "How's school been? You working this whole week or you getting to play some too? Hey Brad, nice to meet you!"

I answered her questions and looked around, wondering where Lollipop was.

"So, um, where's Lollipop?" I asked as I dipped my hand in the popcorn bowl.

"Oh, he's in a bad way, Josie," she said, coming to sit next to me on the couch.

She began to tell me how, shortly after Christmas, Lollipop had started having spells and had needed to be hospitalized. It was the usual with him; the demons of all he had lived through just overwhelmed him at times, and with the holidays and winter settling in, he just didn't have the coping skills. He had been found several times on the streets and was being taken to the shelters for help, but it had just gotten too out of control. The shelters had brought him to the veteran's hospital for a few days and weeks of treatments. He had been there most of the winter. None of them had really seen him much at all.

"Oh, goodness, maybe we can plan a visit?" Brad said.

My heart just swelled when I heard things like that. He didn't even know these folks, yet he had somehow become attached to them just through my stories and these brief minutes of meeting them.

"Sure! That would be fantastic!" Green Leaf said. He said he had been able to catch a cab down to see him a few times, but the cabs were very expensive. The veteran's hospital was a few towns away, and it took all his money just to get there and back each time. I think Green Leaf must have missed him the most. Martin and Girlie seemed to hang out together often, and Bonkers just seemed disconnected enough to not make a difference. But Green Leaf was very sensitive and connected with his family and seemed the most affected by Lollipop's distress in life. I would make it happen. We would go see him in the next few days before I had to return to campus.

Friday Night

· ·

We decided to do something very different Friday night. Brad and I wanted to take a ride into the city and see my campus and have dinner and decided it might be fun to make it a special night for my friends since they had hosted me twice at the cabin. I asked my mom if we could borrow the van to accommodate the extra people and bring them to Round the Table for dinner. Brad and I would spend that much on just us going out to dinner, so why not bring them somewhere they could feel comfortable and perhaps even find a way to get them to work a few shifts at some point? It was a long way for them to come on their own, but maybe during my break when I continued to volunteer, I could arrange to get them in there with me.

So we arrived at Round the Table about a half hour after it had opened, and there was already a line out the door of folks and families waiting to get in. We stood for a bit in line and took turns walking over to the dock area to view the waterfront. It was a beautiful spring night, and I couldn't help but smile as I looked at Martin, Girlie, Green Leaf, and Bonkers all dressed up for dinner. They looked like regular people, not homeless. If homeless even had a look? Here at Round the Table, you really never knew who was who. It just made me feel so warm to be a part of it all.

Dinner was awesome and having told them it was on us, Martin looked at the cards included with our bill for dinner. The four of them discussed coming back and even had our waiter come back to talk about how they could work it out, being able to come back when I returned home. I promised them I would continue my scheduled shifts, and they would all be the first ones I called when I was coming in for one.

We then drove back toward home and made our way to the Veteran's Hospital to see Lollipop. We entered the hospital, looking quite dapper from our dinner out, and walked to the front desk to ask what room our friend was in. We were directed to the fourth floor. Martin and Girlie's eyes met and a knowing nod was exchanged between them. Green Leaf seemed awfully quiet as we rode up in the elevator. I sensed they knew something I was unaware of. As the elevator slowed to a stop at the fourth floor, Bonkers cleared his throat and said, "I think we need to inform Miss Josie and Mr. Brad this is the crazy floor. It might not be easy to see some of the things that go on here, just so you know."

"Oh, well, I . . . I . . . I kind of figured," I stammered. I knew Lollipop was being treated for mental issues and was having treatments to help with his depression, but I didn't really realize he was considered crazy.

"It's just a formality, Josie. It's where he has to be put in order to get the medications and assistance he needs. It's not quite like the movies," Green Leaf said to me, seeing the panic on my face.

"Well, I'm ready if you all are," I said as the elevator doors opened.

We found Lollipop's room easily. It was right outside the nurse's station. Another formality I was assured. It did not mean he was any more in danger than anyone else here Green Leaf told me.

We knocked on the door and said "hello?" as we peered into the semi-dark room. We could hear music playing, and Lollipop singing from the bathroom.

Green Leaf knocked on the bathroom door, "Hey, handsome, you better be decent when you come out! You've got company!"

The door opened, and Lollipop smiled from ear to ear. "Well, look what the cat dragged in! How the heck are you all doing? Gosh, I thought I'd never see you all again! Come, sit down, sorry I only got the one chair."

We sat on the chair, the arm of the chair, the window sill, the other bed in the room, and on the floor. Lollipop turned his radio down and said again, "Gosh, it's good to see some friendly faces! Everyone around here is *crazy*!" He put his finger to his ear and twirled it around and crossed his eyes."

"Is there a sun room or visiting room we can go to?" Girlie asked politely.

Lollipop pressed the call button on his nurses remote and asked, "Is it okay if Sergeant Lollipop heads to the visitation quarters?"

"Of course you may, sir. Over and out." came a crackling voice from the nurse's remote.

Lollipop saluted the remote and hung it back on the side table. We followed him to the end of the hall to the visitation room. We made ourselves comfortable on the couches and opened the bag of dessert we had brought for him.

"Oh wow! My favorite! Cheesecake with strawberries! Thanks, everyone!" and he dug into it. With his mouth full of cheesecake, he asked what we had all been up to, and we told him about our night out at the cabin, visiting my campus and our dinner at Round the Table. He smiled through it all and kept saying he was working real hard to get better, so he could join us soon. Summer was tough he said. It got real hot, and he always broke out in sweats and heard more noises than in the winter. And it brought him right back to the war and all the sights, sounds, and feelings that haunted him. Summer nights were the worst for him, he said, but he was determined this year to break out of it and become whole again. The summer was always worse than his post-holidays winter spell.

"My therapist says I'm doing real good, making great progress with those damn demons. They just sneak up on me, and I can't figure out why."

"You're going to break this. I can feel it," Martin said. "But right now this is the best and safest place for you to be, my friend."

We had a nice visit, Brad showed him pictures of Harvey and promised the next time he would bring him and hopefully by then Lollipop would be out of here, and Harvey could come and run around at the cabin with him. Animals were the best therapy, so we all agreed that would be a great time for him.

The drive home was very animated. Everyone seemed happy to have been able to see Lollipop and enjoy the fantastic dinner together. Brad and I dropped them off at the cabin and said goodbye. I would be back for Easter, but that would only be for the day. So I doubted I would have a chance to visit and then it was right into the final weeks of the school year.

Nobody could believe already one full year had gone by since I started this amazing journey.

Early May

It hardly seemed possible I had only two weeks left to my first year of college. With final projects, final exams, and everyone trying to wrap up the year and get summer jobs lined up, we hardly had time to hang out. But Samantha, Kelsie, and I remained disciplined and went for a jog nearly every afternoon after classes. We always ran along the waterfront and near Round the Table. By now, we were regulars and knew the other regulars. As the days got warmer and longer, we would see the families out there on the dock playing while they waited for their table. Some nights, they were eating outside, and we would stop for a quick chat.

"You girls are so inspiring to us all," one of the moms who we saw on a regular basis said to us one night.

"Aw . . . You inspire us!" I smiled back.

"I just wish I had the opportunities you have when I was your age, if I had gone to school and got a degree, I think my life would be so different. I wouldn't be livin' in the shelter and trying to make ends meet for these two. I tell them every day, Ms. Josie, Ms. Kelsie, and Ms. Samantha are smart girls. You be like them. Don't be like your foolish old mama and throw your life away on some man who says he's gonna make you a wonderful life. You gotta make your *own* way in this world."

Her two children looked at her with big eyes. Then they looked at us with even bigger eyes. It seemed like a nice thing to say, but I didn't feel right about these children thinking their mother was worthless. How could I turn this around and make them feel like their mom was a super hero? I reached out and tucked the youngest one's hair back from her face and said, "Not to worry. You have a pretty cool mom right here, showing you everything you need to know in life. She brings you here, right? And here at Round the Table, it's all about helping each other out. Sure, you are going to have to work hard in life and sure you are going to have to make your own way, but when you've got good people and good friends around you, it's not so hard. All you have to do is ask when you need help and offer to help when you see someone in need."

"Aw, Ms. Josie . . ." Their mom wiped away a tear.

"Ms. Josie," the little girl smiled up at me, "I love you."

"Me too!" said her little brother. "But Mommy is the most beautiful woman ever!"

"Of course she is." I smiled back and patted him on the head.

Kelsie and Samantha brought ice cream over to the kids, and we all walked along the board walk, looking at the boats and pointing to which one we would own one day.

"This will be my yacht," said Samantha. "Once I retire from running the biggest most glamorous hotel chain on the east coast, and I am filthy rich, that is!"

"And I will be your partner in crime, travelling the world with not a care in the world," Kelsie said. "That is, after I sell my fabulously successful chain of upscale restaurants!"

"I'm going to be a pirate! But only a good pirate!" Jimmy said, waving his arms around as if swashbuckling a sword, one eye closed and limping like he had a wooden leg. "A good pirate who steals from bad, rich people to give money to the poor who really need it. *Arrr!* He waved his arms around a bit more and hopped along the boardwalk.

"Well, I'm going to live on that little boat over there and be a fisherwoman," said Jimmy's sister Tessie. "I'm going to fish all day long, and when I get home, I will make myself a fabulously healthy fish dinner and make enough to take to the neighbors and my mom who will be very old and probably very sick by then. I'll make fish dinners for everyone, and they will be magic and make everyone live forever!"

It was great to hear the kids telling their hopes and dreams.

"Which one will you live on, Ms. Josie? Don't you like boats?" Tessie came to take my hand and walk along beside me.

"Oh, I do, but I think I'd rather have just a small boat that I can sail around on when I have a day off. I don't think I want to live on the water or on a boat. I think I'd rather live by a lake or a river and just have a small boat."

"That's our Josie, always making her dreams attainable," Kelsie laughed.

"And of course, Brad will be with you, right?" Samantha said. And they both rolled their eyes and smiled as they said together, "But of course!"

JUNE 1

··

And so began another summer. I was able to work at the coffee shop full time and had been promoted to shift leader. My first week meant lots of training for shift leader, and I had hardly any time to skip out back to see if Martin or any of the others were around.

My boss said she had seen them around more now that the warm weather was here and that they had been looking good. She said they seemed to be getting plenty to eat, and I wondered if they had been spending more time at the shelter. While I was glad they were and I knew eventually one day they would find a way to work back into the reality of society and give up their life on the streets, it sort of made me sad to think I wouldn't see them every day. Living on the streets had to be taking its toll on all of them. None of them were really young, and it wasn't healthy for them to be living like this; that was just plain obvious. I was glad to know they had the cabin to go to and the shelter, but I wanted so much for them to have a place to live and find a job to support themselves. I decided it would be my mission by the end of the summer to do that for at least Martin. If I could get him mainstreamed back to living in society and being a responsible member with a job and place to live, he could maybe inspire the others.

By the end of the week, I was finally able to sit outside on my break and enjoy some time outside alone. I sat with my iced coffee scrolling through my phone and surfing the web when a familiar voice called, "Hello there! Back for the summer, I see?"

It was Martin, the voice was Martin, but I had to look again! My goodness, he was cleaned up and wearing jeans with a polo shirt.

His hair was much shorter, and his eyes were actually sparkling. Sunglasses rested on his head.

"Martin! *Woa!* You look like a million bucks!" I gasped.

"Well, maybe $400 a week, but not a million yet!" He laughed.

I couldn't believe it; he had gone to job services at the shelter and found a job and was working as a teller at the bank in town. With his past history, he had to start all over again, but the teller job also included several customer service aspects, and he was doing a lot to help out the new tellers. He was currently training to be the trainer for the new employees, even though he had only worked there for two months. He was positively beaming and glowing as he told the story about how he found the job, and they were willing to give him a chance. The people at the shelter got him cleaned up and offered services to go and help with the HR things that a man of his ability had but just had a hard time explaining where he had been and why he had been there for the past few years.

"I'm earning a salary again. Not even a respectable amount to rent an apartment, but thankfully the folks at job services also have connections to apartments and homes where people like me can live. They take a certain percent of my salary, and I am expected to give back by helping around the grounds of the apartment complex. It's the first time in my life I actually *hope* I don't get a raise or a bonus, so I can keep my rent low and try to save a bit. But gosh it feels good to have my own money again!"

I was so happy; I thought my cheeks would burst from smiling. Then he told me about Girlie. She had also connected with job services at the shelter and was working part-time at the local grocery store. She was earning less salary, so she had taken a room at the shelter's outreach center. It was a home the shelter had purchased and used for women who were getting back on their feet. Currently four families and three single women lived there. All of them were expected to help out with expenses, food, and upkeep of the house. It was like one big extended family. He said Girlie never seemed happier. She had children around and offered to babysit when the moms needed to work. It was her way to help and give back. Working part-time at the grocery store, and babysitting filled a need and filled her with purpose. Having never had her own children, she desperately needed to feel that bond.

Wow. My cheeks were really going to burst from pride in my friends. I felt like my own children had fledged the nest. My heart was so full. I couldn't wait to tell Brad!

I realized my boss had been sneaky when she told me she had seen them around a bit more, saying the warm weather was what brought them around. It wasn't the warm weather at all! It was that they stopped by on their way to work or on their way home from work! Working just down the street at the bank and at the grocery store at the other end of town, they had time and money to stop and get a cup of coffee once in a while.

Later That Week

Was I surprised to see Martin standing in line early one morning!

"Well, good morning, sir!" I smiled at him. He smiled back, but his eyes did not smile. I immediately sensed something was terribly wrong.

"Martin, what is it?" I had to lean close to hear him, he spoke so softly.

"Lollipop is in a bad way, Josie," he said. I could see the pain on his face. "And Green Leaf won't leave him; he's been at the hospital for two days straight.

I felt myself go cold with fear. *What did he mean by in a bad way?* I wondered. I turned to ask my boss if I could take a quick five minute break. She knew by the look on my face and the concern on Martin's that something had to be wrong for me to ask and granted me the five minutes, hurrying to cover the register for me.

"What is going on?" I asked Martin as I came around the counter.

"He took some drugs, Josie. He just took some drugs. He's in a coma, and they have him hooked up to all sorts of machines. It doesn't look good. Damn, he was doing so well too!"

"Surely it must have been a mistake, Martin?" I asked, wiping away a tear that slid down my cheek.

"Well, we just don't know. Green Leaf found him at the cabin, asleep in the chair, but he wasn't asleep. He was unconscious. By the time they got to the main house to call the ambulance, too much time may have passed. Nobody knows how long he was really out for. There was a bottle next to him with his prescription, but it looks like he may have mixed that with something else. God, I hope he pulls through. He was doing so well. We can't lose him."

"I have to get back, my boss said five minutes. Martin, come by at lunch, and we'll call the hospital and see if we can get an update on him, okay?"

Martin left with his coffee, his shoulders a bit slumped. I hoped this wouldn't cause him to slip back into bad habits and upset the job he had found. We were all so happy just a few weeks ago. How could this happen?

One Week Later

Lollipop remained in a coma for the entire week. Going on day ten, we learned there probably was no hope for him to come out of it. We all sat around his bed, wishing he would wake up and smile at us. But his big smile had gone, and it seemed the life, tormented as it was, had gone from him too. His family had also come to sit and wait. They were remarkable people; they had tried so hard to keep him from the life that claimed him so easily. The darkness of the demons he had witnessed had eventually became too strong for him. We sat around telling our favorite stories about him. Several times we swore we saw him flinch: a fleeting smile or a twitch of a finger, but the doctors confirmed it was just tricks our minds were playing. He was gone, and at this point, it was senseless to try to keep him alive.

I asked his sister, "How did he get the name Lollipop?" as we sat watching him. He looked so peaceful; it was hard to realize that in his moment of death, he finally found the peace his mind had searched for all this time.

"He got the name when he was a teenager. While all the other kids began sneaking cigarettes from their parents, Lewis started always sucking on a lollipop. He'd keep the stick in his mouth for hours after the pop was gone. So we started calling him Lollipop."

I remembered he had one in his mouth the day I met him!

"His real name is Lewis?" I smiled through my tears. I had never known.

Lewis Fredrick Jones. Sergeant Lewis Frederick Jones as the U.S. Army knew him.

She told me he had been the happiest baby anyone had ever seen. His mother swore he never cried a day in his life. He always had a smile on his face, a kind word to say and was there to help anyone who needed it. Even though things didn't always come easy, he was the happiest kid around. He wasn't the smartest kid in class, but he always tried the hardest. Nothing could beat his giant personality down—not bullies at school, not bigger kids on the bus, not teachers who told him he would never make it out of school. He'd just smile back and say, "It's okay. I'm a good person with a big heart. That's all that matters in this life."

Nothing could beat him down.

Until he joined the Army and went off to fight in the war.

All he ever wanted in life was do the right thing and have a family. He thought doing the right thing was joining the service and fighting for his country. He was so proud to wear the uniform and serve with his unit.

"But he came back changed, Josie, he really did. That big personality wasn't there anymore. It was like someone took what was inside him that made him who he was and just ripped it out. His eyes always looked so sad. He rarely slept. And when he did sleep, the night terrors that took over consumed him. He would wake up yelling and screaming, drenched in sweat and calling out names of people we had only heard about in letters and e-mails that came home while he was off fighting. Many of the names were men from his unit that were killed when one of the tanks they were in hit a hidden explosive device and he watched the tank blow up right in front of him in the convoy. All of them were killed instantly. Lewis would never talk about it, but he said over and over he held such guilt for not being one of the ones killed. He always said he should have been one of the ones to die."

His sister told me so much about him. He had wanted to have a family but after all the issues he had from returning, he just never felt he could offer anyone the stability that would be needed to be a good husband and father. And that began the downward spiral of depression, drugs and homelessness. His family tried tirelessly to keep him above it all, but it just had such a grip on his mind.

"I would give anything to see that happy kid, smiling and sucking on a lollipop stick," his sister sobbed as she held his lifeless hand.

I watched as she rubbed his hand and sobbed into the tissues she held. I wanted to leave and leave her alone but also felt I should stay for support.

"Goodbye, Lollipop. I love you forever."

And she got up and left the room.

I was left alone with him. The hiss of the machines, his lifeless body, and my mind racing a thousand miles a minute.

I heard the door creak open and saw Martin, Girlie, Bonkers, and Green Leaf peering in.

"It's time," I said through my tears.

We all gathered around the bed and took our turns saying goodbye to Lollipop. We knew it was time to go and let his family have their last few minutes with him as they turned off the life support machines. Somehow it felt like we were saying goodbye to a member of our own family. We all stood there in a crescent at the side of his bed, tears flowing freely but knowing he was finally free. His body would fail, but his mind would be forever free and happy again. He would go back to that carefree, smiling healthy person he once was with a lollipop in his mouth. He would always be our Lollipop.

We turned to leave and met Brad walking in. He came over and hugged me as the rest of us clung to each other, moving away from the bed and toward the door.

"Brad! Thank you so much for being here!" I gave him a sloppy tear-filled kiss.

Green Leaf turned and saluted Sergeant Lewis Frederick Jones and said, "Sleep well, our friend. Sleep well."

We exchanged looks and hugs with his family members out in the hall, knowing this would be our last visit here. They said they had a memorial service planned for the next week, and we said we would see them there.

As we walked the hall to the elevator, the nurses and a couple of doctors gave us silent nods, knowing there was nothing they could say that could change what was about to happen but knowing their hearts were heavy along with ours.

Sometimes finding common ground hurt. The bonds of the heart were strong to bind us all together, but it also felt like a vice—ripping our hearts apart.

MONDAY

My first week of summer and training done, I began taking on some of the supervisor roles I was now trained for. About halfway through my first shift, my boss's boss came in for a visit. She looked surprised to see him and said, "I'll be right with you. We can talk in the office."

"That's very nice, but I'm not here to see you. I'm here to see Josie."

The look on my boss's face must have mirrored mine. Nothing short of a deer in headlights look on both of our faces. My heart began to pound. I had just been promoted to supervisor, so surely he wasn't planning to fire me for the way I spoke with him the last time we met. He must know I was being promoted and would have said something to my boss before this.

He motioned for me to come to the office with him. My boss jumped behind the counter to cover for me.

When we got to the office, he motioned to a chair for me to sit, and he sat behind the desk.

"Josie, the last time I was here, I felt like you made some very good points. At the time, I didn't really think much of them or you, to be honest with you."

I recalled our conversation ending with me not being sure if he was mocking me or accepting some of my ideas.

"I wrote down several of your ideas, and although I have to say, due to corporate regulations, we cannot do some of them, I am willing to try a few ideas. I would like to start with a children's story hour and Wi-Fi free night. As our newest supervisor and visionary, I would like to put you in charge of it. I'll give you until Thursday to write up a proposal, and we'll go from there."

"Oh, sir!" I wanted to jump up and hug him, but I knew that was totally inappropriate. I already had ideas going in my head. I could see it now, the Wi-Fi off, just families and children in the shop with carpets on the floor around the fire and guest readers reading books to the kids or story tellers telling stories. Sunday evening would be perfect. It was always the slowest time of the week, and it wouldn't be too late for the kids. They could even come in their pajamas if they wanted! I was just thrilled to be given the chance and that he was willing to listen to some of the ideas I had.

We had found some common ground.

Common ground, it was easy even when you weren't trying. You just had to keep the faith as Nana would say.

"Okay, Josie, I see you have ideas cooking already. Your excitement and vision is truly amazing and infectious. I can't wait to hear what you have planned.

Dare I tell him I wanted my first guest reader to be Martin? He never had his own children, and I was thinking this was the perfect way for him to connect and give to some children what he never could with his own. Would this corporate representative see the former homeless man as more than someone who searched the dumpster for food? Would he see beyond that to the man he once was and working hard to become again in some way? Would he see that regardless of our circumstances, we all have value and something to offer?

I couldn't wait to talk with Martin and my friend at the library and get something going for some story hours. Maybe I could even talk Brad into coming to read a book to the kids and talk about astronomy! This was magical to me. From such a low point last week, saying goodbye to Lollipop, to this. I could feel my future taking shape.

Thursday

I got to work a half hour early mainly because I just could not sleep any later and had been up reviewing my proposal since 5:00 a.m. I had talked with Martin about coming to read to the kids, and he was thrilled I had asked him. He said the first book he would bring to read was his wife's favorite children's book. It was one she had bought when they thought they were pregnant the first time and had it sitting on the shelf in what would become the nursery. When she lost the first baby, he said he would often find her sitting in the room on the floor reading the book, tears flowing down her cheeks. It was a sweet story about being loved and growing to become the best person ever. It was meant for a parent to read to a child, and it was just so fitting that she had wanted to read it to her own child one day. After losing three babies and the long spans in between of not getting pregnant, he said she just packed everything away and never looked at it again. It was one of the few things Martin kept with him when he lost everything. He had it packed away in a backpack he kept at the cabin.

"I should really get that and bring it to my new place, but somehow that cabin has just always felt like home to me since I started staying there. After dragging all I owned around in one backpack for so many years from place to place, I felt I finally belonged somewhere and wanted my things there."

I then talked with my friend who worked at the local library and got some ideas for books to read, and she kindly said she would spread the word to some of the librarians and see if some of them would volunteer to be guest readers. She also suggested I get in touch with Miss Molly, the local colorful storyteller who did a weekly story hour at the historical center about the history of the town, local events, and the various holidays throughout the year. She was great. She had costumes and props, and the children mostly knew her from school so they would love to see her, I was sure.

If the big boss accepted my idea, Sunday evenings would become Sunday Story Hour for the local children. We would light the fireplace and serve cocoa, apple cider, and snacks while the children sat on carpets donated by my mother's friend who owned the local interior decorating agency. She always had swatches around the office; it was easy to get her to give up a dozen or so for a good cause.

My boss loved the ideas and said it was a no brainer: although Sunday afternoons typically were very slow, this would bring in some business and make it worthwhile to stay open the extra few hours they had been considering taking off the schedule. We would go Wi-Fi free for the two hours, so the parents would be engaged with the children. Without Wi-Fi, there wouldn't be many other patrons, so the children would be comfortable to be free and act like children.

It was all coming together. Next I had to talk with Brad about a special idea I had planned for the last night of summer before I went back to school.

I couldn't be more pleased with the way things were going at the coffee shop for me.

Friday

I had requested the day off to attend Lollipop's memorial service. His family felt it was only right to have a small service at the farm. It was where he had been most comfortable and was really beginning to find the peace and serenity he needed for his mind. He was at ease on the land and in the little cabin. It had become home to him and his friends were his family.

His body had been cremated, and the service was simple. We each took turns saying a few words about him and sharing stories about his life. Sometimes it was quite humorous; other times, it was just sad to think he was never going to be with us. Knowing he was at peace, we scattered his ashes in the back of the farm, at the base of the hills. As the wind took the ashes and we watched the specks float and then settle on the land, we knew Lollipop was finally at peace. His mind could rest, and he would no longer be tormented by the demons of his mind.

Rest in peace, Sergeant Lewis Frederick Jones.

Green Leaf saluted. Girlie wiped her final tears. Martin bowed his head and was muttering a prayer, and Bonkers stood with his hat over his heart. I glanced at this group of people, and my heart was full. Broken and empty yet full all at the same time.

The next week flew by as summer was in full swing in my home town. The coffee shop was the hub of activity for busy moms and their kids, business men and women, and college kids who liked to hang out and use the Wi-Fi for connecting. I was thrilled to see many moms stop to read the poster we had placed in the front window about the first Sunday Story Hour. Many of them made a note in their phone, and I heard several of them telling their children how fun it was going to be. Hopefully we'd have at least a dozen to fill the little squares of carpet I had!

The Next Sunday

We closed the shop officially at 4:00 p.m. in order to prepare the area for the kids. We had planned chocolate chip cookies and apple juice for the first time. By 5:00 p.m., we were ready to have our first Sunday Story Hour and re-opened the doors. I couldn't believe when I went to unlock the door and saw a mob outside! There were at least twenty children with their parents standing out there! Some had their PJs on, and everyone was excited.

"Welcome, everyone! I have a few carpets for you to sit on, and others feel free to grab some room on the couches! Mr. Martin will be reading tonight, and he is already over by the fireplace. Go ahead and get settled, and we'll begin in just a few minutes."

Oh my goodness, I never expected so many! As we settled in and began passing out cookies and juice my boss lit a few candles in the fireplace. The night was too warm for a fire, but the candles added a special glow to the room. She placed the safety screen in front and took her place on the stones in front of the fireplace, making sure none of the children got close enough to touch the candles.

I heard the door open, and three more families came in and settled in. Wow! This was great. I just wished the big boss was here to see this.

Martin began to read, and he was a huge hit! He was so animated and made all these funny voices of each character that the children were silent as church mice. Most of them even forgot they had cookies and juice and just sat silent, listening to the adventures Martin was taking them on. He had brought the special book his wife so loved and also brought several more. Once he started, he read five books to the children. Most of them were so captivated by his reading they didn't notice their parents had gotten up to get coffee at the counter and were now sitting in the back together. The hour flew by, and everyone was asking if this was going to be every Sunday. They wanted more! My boss was giddy, and I saw her glance over near the door and back to the parents, "Of course! Next Sunday it is!"

I followed her eyes to the door and saw her boss standing there. He grinned at me and gave a thumbs up.

I tried to stifle my smile, but I couldn't help but grin like a Cheshire cat! *This* was how I pictured my life to be. One day, when I owned my own coffee shop, I hoped to have this many people there and all being as happy as this.

MONDAY

Brad was coming to visit, and I wanted to get some extra food for the house before he got there. My mom and I planned a special barbecue dinner with some friends and family to meet him during this visit. As I was putting my items on the belt at the register, I realized Girlie was my cashier. I hadn't yet seen her at work, and it was good to see her there! She seemed at ease and very happy. Usually, when she was around Martin and the other guys, she was fairly quiet and let them do most of the talking, but here she was chatting with nearly every customer who went through her line. It seemed she knew most of them, even though she had only been working there a few weeks. Her nearly toothless smile and her happy chatter was just what I needed this Monday morning. It had been a fun weekend, but I was tired from the Sunday Story Hour at the shop and all the preparation I had done. As I got closer, Girlie saw me and gave me a big smile. Toothless or not, her smile could light up a room!

We chatted a bit about the service for Lollipop and how fitting it had been: simple and poignant, much like him it seemed. Although none of us knew him most of his life, we all felt like we had gotten to know him during the last few days of his life through his family's stories about his life.

I told Girlie about all the children who had come to Sunday Story Hour at the shop and her eyes lit up.

"Oh, maybe I can bring some of the children from my home to the next one?" Her eyes twinkled. I could tell she was already very smitten with most of them, and I was sure they felt the same way about her.

"Of course you can, we are planning another one this Sunday, and Martin has agreed to read again this week. Bring as many children as you would like!"

"That would be great. I love spending time with these kids, and they are all just too cute and too precious. And it gives their parents a nice break," Girlie winked at me.

"Great, if I don't see you before that, I'll see you Sunday!"

I pushed my cart to the car and loaded the groceries in. I couldn't wait to see Brad. I had not seen him in several weeks, and although we talked everyday on the phone or with FaceTime, I missed being with him. And I missed Harvey.

Monday Afternoon

Mom and I got the salad made and began cutting up some fruit for a fruit salad as Dad and Brad pulled the marinated meat from the refrigerator to start the barbecue. Family and friends had begun to arrive and were congregating in the kitchen and out in the yard. Harvey was busy pacing, following anyone he thought had food that might be dropped. His nose in the air, his eyes pinpointed on whoever he was following, hopeful drool hanging off his lips.

"Quite a picture of beauty, Harvey!" I laughed as I stepped around him to put the salads on the table.

Brad came back inside with the dirty pans from the meat and announced, "T-minus fifteen minutes, Harvey! Dinner will be served in fifteen minutes. Think you can wait that long, buddy?" He scratched under his chin, and Harvey licked furiously at his hands, hoping just maybe for a taste of the delicious sauce.

"Hey, Brad," I asked as I stirred a pitcher of iced tea. "I was wondering if you might be interested in being the star of my last Summer Sunday Story Hour at the shop? No pun intended. By star I mean, maybe you could read something to the kids about astronomy, the constellations, and stuff like that?"

"Sure! I'd love to! Just tell me the date, and I'm there!"

I knew he would say yes; he was too good to me.

"And dinner is served! Come and get it!" Dad called from outside. Everyone made their way to the tables on the patio. It was a beautiful summer night.

I wasn't sure, at this point in my life, if I could have asked for a more perfect life.

WEDNESDAY

Getting back to work after several days off was tough, but I didn't have time to really think about any of that. Right when I walked in, I learned we had two people out sick: One had a horrible sunburn from her day at the beach the day before, and another had broken her ankle by falling off her bike. We had tried to call people in to replace them, but between vacations and other plans, nobody was available. It was just go, go, go all morning. I looked up at one point and saw Girlie standing in line. I waved and smiled at her. I just couldn't believe her transformation from last summer at this time, the woman I met out back by the dumpster looking disheveled and frumpy, to the slightly scattered woman who stood before me waiting to buy a coffee. I was so proud of how far she had come.

When she got up to the counter, she ordered her coffee and said, "I wanted to come by and see you, Josie. I have some good news to share. I've gone full-time at the store starting next week and that means I will begin having medical benefits. The first thing I'm going to do is look into having my teeth fixed."

"Oh, Girlie! I'm so happy for you! You have such a beautiful smile. It's going to get even better once you have some pearly whites to flash there!"

I handed her coffee to her. Under the little nymph on side of the cup, instead of writing "Girlie," I drew a big happy face with extra large teeth, like the emoji that were so popular.

Her eyes twinkled and she giggled. "I know! I'll look so much younger too, don't you think? Maybe I'll find a man!" We both laughed, and she took her cup and waved to me as she walked out.

The summer was flying by, and I realized I had not seen Green Leaf since we had been out to the farm for Lollipop's service. I decided I would take a ride out after work and see if he was around. Brad was visiting for the rest of the week, so after I got done at the coffee shop, I stopped by the house to see if he wanted to take a ride out and try to see Green Leaf.

"Sure, come on, Harvey!" and we all jumped in the car.

We got to the farm and parked near the cabin. I wondered if Green Leaf was still staying there, even though Martin and Girlie had moved on. Just then, Bonkers came around from the side of the cabin with a large bucket of corn.

"Hey there, you two! Long time no see!" he shaded his eyes from the sun.

"Hey, Bonkers!" we waved.

Harvey picked up a stick and began to circle us, trying to get anyone, someone to throw the stick and play fetch. Bonkers grabbed the stick and threw it way out into one of the fields. Harvey ran after it, barking the whole way, happy to have some space to run!

"Bonkers, how are you and Green Leaf doing? We haven't seen you in a while," I asked.

"Oh, doing great! Gosh, Green Leaf put me to work out here! Feels so good to have my hands in the dirt and something to *do*! We planted all that corn, and over there, we have some tomatoes, peppers, eggplant, cucumbers, and squash. We've got pumpkins over there and even some lettuce, but the darn rabbits mostly got that whole crop. We're having some good luck with the vegetables, and Lollipop's sister has a beautiful wild flower garden out by her house. So between our vegetables and her flowers, we're having us a great time selling stuff out on Route 9. The guy out there has a stand and takes some of our stuff, sells it, and gives us the profit. He knows we don't have no way to get out there, so he comes here and gets it from us. All he takes is the money for the gas to get out here."

"Oh, wow! You guys have a business going! Well, isn't that great! No wonder we haven't seen much of you!"

Harvey sat next to me, his tail pounding on my leg, patiently waiting for me to throw the stick again.

Harvey started to run and someone whistled. He stopped and looked the other way, confused. He looked in the direction I threw the stick and the whistle came again. Harvey started to run then sat down, his head cocked to the side.

We looked to where he was looking and saw Green Leaf standing by the path leading to the house behind the cabin, laughing and trying to whistle again.

"I wish I could read your thoughts, Harvey!" he said. Harvey ran to him and jumped up, licking his face.

Green Leaf was filthy from his day working in the garden. But he was also very tan and healthy looking. I was so happy for him. I knew he missed Lollipop more than the rest of us, and I was glad he had found something to occupy himself with.

"I have even better news," he said, taking a towel from his pocket and wiping his face.

"There is a small restaurant in the next town, and the owner asked me if I could cook a bit for him this fall. His cook is going to be out on medical leave for a few months, and he's up the creek. Somehow, he found out I know a thing or two about cooking, and he asked me if I'd be interested. Darned if I can figure out how he found out I can cook, but what the heck, right? If he thinks I can help him, well, who am I to say no?"

Bonkers grinned and put a finger to his lips. He winked and pointed at his chest. I smiled back, knowing they had been looking out for each other these past few weeks.

"Go 'head, Bonkers, now tell 'em your news." Green Leaf said.

"Aw, heck, mine ain't much, just a guy having some fun with a can of paint, that's all," he said and pushed his foot around in the dirt, like a kid embarrassed with telling his mother something.

"Oh it is *Not* at all! *This* guy here has been *hired* by the town to help paint the new mural on the bridge coming into town!" Green Leaf put his arm around Bonkers, and they both grinned like boys caught with their fingers in the cookie jar.

"What? You have been?" Brad and I said in unison.

Harvey thumped his tail against Brad's leg again.

Green Leaf couldn't hold back and, like a proud parent, told us how it all came to be that Bonkers was going to help paint the mural.

There had been a contest held, and folks were asked to submit a sample of their drawing, painting, or a sketch depicting the history of our town. Green Leaf had asked Bonkers to draw something, telling him he thought maybe they could put up a few pictures in the cabin and secretly submitted it.

"Wait, you can paint or draw?" I asked Bonkers.

"Aw. Heck yeah! Back in the day, I taught art at the school. I was the crazy dude that everyone said hung out in the pottery area too long or sniffed too much paint, glue, and other creative substances. I'm the genuine thing, creative free spirit at your service."

Woa! Bonkers had been a teacher? Why had we never known this before?

"Yup, it's true. I was a crazy art teacher back in the day. Then one day, I just snapped. I don't know why, I just had a complete breakdown, and I was let go. I went from being a crazy free spirit to being a crazy free spirit with no job. I just sort of spiraled down. I never really "fit" into society anyway; it was easy to just let it all go. But I missed the kids. The kids were why I did it. I loved watching those little minds realize what they had locked in there and how to let it out. I loved watching the creativity brew, bubble up, and *bam!* They had something they could be proud of! But it all went away. The crazy free spirit was now someone everyone was afraid of, shied away from, and looked the other way when I came near. I wasn't a crazy free spirit anymore, I was just plain crazy."

It was all sort of sad to me. We had called him Bonkers, thinking it was funny the way he acted and the way he seemed, well, bonkers. But, it stemmed from a serious break down.

"Don't let it get you down, Josie, I'm good now. I take my medication, and I still have that crazy free spirit in me. I just use it for good now. And I still miss the kids. I'm hoping once the town sees what I can do with a can of paint that somehow it will all come back to me."

"Amen," Green Leaf said.

Harvey thumped his tail again. Brad bent to pick up the stick.

My mind began to head into overdrive. Kids. Paint. I think I had an idea or two.

Wednesday Night

I hadn't been keeping up with my journal and realized I had learned so many precious things in just this year that would take me far in life. After watching a movie with Brad and my parents, I pulled the book out and began to write some things that I wanted to remember for one day when I had my own coffee shop. Things I had learned about business, people, and just being respectful and dignified. I've always known respect is something you earn. If you don't give respect, you don't get respect. And that was the main lesson I would take into life and my coffee shop.

I had also learned dignity. When you act dignified and treat others with dignity, you are already in a better place. In life or a coffee shop, it didn't matter which side of the counter you were on. What matters is that you see and know who you are with.

The quality of your personality and character reflected back in the quality of your product.

"Serve up quality, and you'll never lack for hearts around your table," Nana's kitchen table philosophy came back to me.

Along with the jottings of coffee basics, I had volumes of notes from my classes, and the business knowledge I had learned was building. I couldn't wait to put it all to the test one day when I truly became my own barista.

July 4

Independence Day was always a big deal in our town. From back in the day when farms covered the outskirts to the small mills that dotted the river running through it, the town was rooted in hard work, families, and community. Watching the times change and the town change was fascinating to me. We still had the beautiful land around the farms, but the mills had become retail businesses, condominium units, and office parks. These architectural pieces were the heart of an era, and it was fascinating to see them keep their integrity while becoming something new for the generations they now served.

The show piece of architectural beauty for our town was the large bridge coming into town. It arched over the river, and the train tracks ran along it high above the road and river. The bridge had been built over a hundred years ago, and over time, it had begun to deteriorate. This was how the idea to paint the mural depicting the town's history had come to be: A team of masons were hired to reface the surfaces just below the train tracks, and the artists were selected by contest to paint the town's history. The unveiling would be Independence Day weekend. In order to unveil it, the town parade was re-routed from the downtown area to the long winding road, leading in and out of town and along the bridge. It seemed everyone had gathered along the route to watch the parade and then meander down to gather just below the bridge to watch the unveiling.

The bridge was dressed in a large black drape for the few days leading up to the holiday and today it would become part of our history. The town manager stood at the top of the bridge above the drape and announced the names of the distinguished artists who had helped to create the mural we all waited to see.

"Ladies and Gentlemen, it is my distinct honor to present to you our newest piece of living history. One that will remind us from where it is we come from and where it is we will we be in the future. It is only through the amazing talent of these four individuals standing beside me that this living piece of art has become reality. From the vision of our past to the prospects of our future, we thank you for your creativity, time, and dedication to who we are. As he named each artist and shook their hands, the crowd clapped and whistled. When Bonker's name was called, he tipped his hat to the crowd and bowed then shook the town manager's hand.

John Joseph McFadden.

This was his moment.

As the black drape was pulled to the side, the crowd let out a collective *aah* as the history of our town came to life. From the first Native Americans who walked the rolling hills to the farmers in the fields. From the rivers and ponds with children playing and the first one-room school house that was now the youth center. From the first church that still stood to the mills where generations had worked and now worked but in vastly different jobs to the newly built sports center. The blend of land, buildings, and the people who built the town was magical. It was a snapshot of living history.

The journalists were there snapping photos and talking to the artists and the crowd, making a story for tomorrow's paper. Ms. Molly was there in costume, chatting with the children and answering their questions about the history of the town. Nobody knew the history of the town better than Ms. Molly!

Bonkers made his way off the bridge and through the crowd. He found Brad and me and was proudly telling us which part of the mural he drew when Martin came up with Girlie.

"Hey there, John Joseph!" he said as he shook his hand.

"Aw, really, I prefer Bonkers. John Joseph was my dad!" Bonkers blushed and shook Martin's hand.

"You've got some beautiful talent, Bonkers," Girlie said smiling at him.

"Aw, thanks, but gosh, you see that kid over there? He's just sixteen years old, and he did all the portraiture! He's got some mad talent, that kid! I wish I had known at sixteen how to channel that. He's got a great future. I bet he'll go to school on a scholarship for art!"

"Maybe you could be some kind of mentor for him?" Girlie said to Bonkers.

Bonkers cocked his head to one side and wrinkled his eyebrows, "You think?"

We all agreed, Bonkers had been a teacher and knew his way around an art studio, and it could be a way to keep him focused and give some purpose to his days. He surely loved art and had great talent.

"You said you miss the kids the most, so why not find a way to get back into it?" I said, forming an idea in my mind.

"I just may. If they'll have me. Whoever they are!" Bonkers laughed.

I knew this would not be the end of Bonkers and his art.

The rest of the day was spent at the town park playing games and having a barbecue. It seemed everyone in town turned out for the festivities this year.

As Brad and I walked around looking at the games to play and talking with friends, Brad grabbed my hand and motioned silently with his eyes to the edge of the park. I saw Girlie and Martin sitting under a tree with two young girls. To a stranger, it would appear to be grandparents out for a picnic with their granddaughters. They sat on a blanket with a picnic basket next to them, sandwiches and drinks in front of each of them. The girls were laughing and eating their sandwiches while Girlie seemed to be telling them a very funny story. We walked closer, and Martin waved. "Come join us! We've got plenty to share!" He waved his hand over the blanket, and we sat down. Girlie introduced us, "These are my friends, Josie and Brad. Josie and Brad, this is Ariel and Lexi. They are joining me today because their mommy isn't feeling too well and needs to stay home.

The girls looked up with their big blue eyes and smiled at us. "Hello!" they said in unison. "It is nice to meet you!"

"Hello," Brad and I said together.

"How's your Fourth of July been so far?" Brad asked the girls.

"Oh, we're having lots of fun, but we wish our mom could be here. She's very sick. She has been very sick a lot lately."

"I'm so sorry to hear that. I hope she gets better soon," Brad said.

Martin looked at me with concern on his face. Somehow I drew the conclusion from his look that their mom was much sicker than they knew.

"Well, goodness, you've just had a wonderful picnic lunch, and you know what always made me feel better when I was a kid?" Brad asked the girls.

"No! What?" the girls said together in anticipation. At this moment, Brad had all the answers in the world. He was like a wizard with a promise of something magical about to be revealed.

"Ice cream!" he shouted and waved his arms. "Who loves ice cream?" he shouted.

"I do! I do!" and two hands shot up in the air.

"Then let's ask if it's okay if we go over there to the ice cream truck and get ourselves the biggest, gooiest, most meltiest, coldest, stickiest ice cream cone he has, huh?"

"Oh, may we?" the girls turned to Girlie who nodded and smiled.

We watched Brad walk off with two bobbing blonde heads, hands all joined and the sun in their eyes as they chattered on about something Brad seemed terribly interested in hearing.

Once out of earshot Martin explained their mom had recently gotten herself hooked on drugs again. She had been shooting heroin and was fired from her job. She was currently technically missing. She had not been home for three days. Her counselor at the home knew where she went when she went on these binges but had not yet been able to track her down. The girls had not seen her in over a week.

"Who has been taking care of them?" I asked with concern.

Martin put his arm around Girlie and said, "This woman right here. She moved them into her apartment and has changed her schedule at the store to be there to get them ready in the morning to go to summer camp. They also have an older sister. She is here somewhere today with her friends. She's thirteen and a lot more aware of her mom's troubles, so we're keeping a close eye on her."

Oh my, Girlie had her hands full, but honestly, I had never seen her look better! She looked healthy and rested and *happy*! Not that she didn't look happy before—she always had her giggles when around Martin, but this seemed to radiate from inside her. She seemed happy from within. I felt oddly at ease with this. I knew their mom was in grave danger, but to be under the care of this wonderful surrogate mother, I just knew they would be okay no matter how circumstances turned out.

Brad and the girls returned just then with ice cream and two very sticky little girls. They also had their big sister and her two friends with them.

"Oh, hi, Vanessa!" Girlie said to their sister.

"Hey," she smiled back.

"This is Ariel and Lexi's big sister, Vanessa. Vanessa, this is Brad's friend, Josie."

"Hey, I know you from the coffee shop on Main Street!" Vanessa said to me.

I had seen her several times with her friends after school. They would come in on their way to the library to get a hot cocoa or cookies. I was happy to see she was one of the kids we never had troubles with. For what the home situation seemed to be, it seemed she was very grounded, a good student, and had a good head on her shoulders. She probably had a lot of responsibility at home, but I was glad she seemed to have someone to share that with.

"Is It okay if I go over Eve's house and go to the fireworks with her family?" she asked Girlie.

"I don't see why not," Girlie said.

"But I'm crushed you don't want to spend time with me!" Martin grinned up at her.

She ran over and gave him a big hug. "You know I'll be there for my bedtime hug, Martin," she said as she bounced off with her friends.

The fireworks were spectacular! I lay on a blanket next to Brad, staring up at the dark sky. As each color burst into twinkling, dancing dots and streaks of light the crowd *oooh'd* and *aaah'd* over and over again. The synchronized bursts were choreographed to fun music, so there was something for everyone. Brad reached over and took my hand.

"This is perfect, isn't it?" he said into the darkness between sparks.

"It is, just perfect." I sighed.

AUGUST 1

The summer was buzzing by faster than a mosquito in the dark on a sultry summer night. Our Sunday Story Hour was turning into the biggest event of the week. Each week we had more children and families than the previous week, and each week, we did something a little different to keep it from becoming too predictable.

The week Girlie brought the children from the home where she lived turned out to be the most fun and most unexpected Story Hour of the summer.

I had scheduled my friend from the library to read that night. She picked a couple of books about butterflies and planned a small activity for the children to do after she read. Working in the children's room and working part-time at a summer camp, she had lots of ideas and supplies that she could easily bring. We had the supplies at the coffee shop, and I was setting up a long table at the back of the shop for the children to do the activity when my friend called to say she couldn't make it tonight. "I feel terrible, but my dad cut his leg, and I need to take him to the hospital for stitches. My mom is out of town, and he can't drive himself. I'm so sorry!"

"No worries, I'll figure something out. I'll read the books myself if I have to!"

"That's the other problem, I brought the craft things, but I forgot the books! I'm really sorry. I don't have time to drop them off."

Oh boy, *that* was a problem. But it was not *her* problem!

"No worry, I'll figure something out, go take care of your dad, and I hope he'll be okay!"

Just then, Girlie walked in with Ariel and Lexi. "Sorry we are early. We were out playing, and I thought I'd stop by and see if you needed any help?"

"Oh, Girlie! I just found out my friend can't read tonight and worse, still, she has the books! I think I'll have to cancel tonight. I feel terrible!"

Girlie looked at the two girls holding her hands. Ariel smiled at me and said, "We can use our books, we have like a gazillion books at our house!"

"They do! These two read all the time, give us a few minutes, and we'll run home and see what we can find!"

"Oh, Girlie! Your timing is amazing!" I gushed.

Ariel then looked back at the table and asked, "What is all that for?"

"Oh, we were going to read about butterflies tonight and then make a butterfly to bring home," I said trying to hide my sadness.

"Butterflies? That's our favorite! We have lots of books about butterflies, and we even have a butterfly net that goes with one of them!" she said with the biggest smile I've ever seen.

"Perfect! Can we borrow them for tonight?" I asked.

"Sure! My big sister can maybe read one. Vanessa is thirteen and can read all the words," the little girl smiled again.

Girlie and the two girls rushed out the door, calling back to me that they would see me soon!

By the time they got back, a few children and families had arrived, and I was getting everyone settled. Since we were running off schedule, I decided to let everyone get their snack first and get that out of the way, so it would all be cleaned up before we started the craft. Too much mess, and I would be here all night cleaning!

Girlie rushed in the door with the two little girls, several books, and their older sister trailing behind. Without missing a beat, she sat in the chair by the fireplace and announced, "Who wants to hear the story of the butterfly who didn't like butter?"

The room became silent as she began to read a very funny story about a butterfly that spent her entire life explaining to people she was not a fly who liked butter but a beautiful butterfly. The story was uproariously funny, and Girlie did the exasperated butterfly voice perfectly. By the end of the story, she had all the children laughing and yelling along with her, "Nooo . . . Nooo . . . I am not a *butter fly*! I am a butterfly!" And she would flap her arms like wings, throw her head back, roll her eyes, and sigh loudly.

Girlie and Vanessa read two more books to the children, and then we started making butterflies out of colorful tissue paper and clothes pins. It was a simple craft, but easy for even the youngest in the group. Everyone left with a treasure to bring home, and we even made a few extras to clip around the coffee shop.

Everyone was asking Girlie if she could read again next week. Her toothless grin and sparkling eyes were thrilling to see. She had a large group of children all around her, like she was a celebrity. She was totally enjoying every moment. I watched as I began to clean up the craft table and sweep the floor. My boss stood by the door, thanking the children and their parents. When the last family left, Girlie let out a loud sigh and plopped down on one of the couches. She fanned herself and exclaimed, "I forgot how tiring children can be!"

"But their enthusiasm is infectious, isn't it?" I said from the back of the room.

Girlie suddenly sat up, like she just remembered I was there.

"Josie! Oh my goodness, I am so sorry, I stole the whole night! I didn't even give you a chance to read!"

It didn't matter to me. Story hour was not my story hour; it belonged to whomever was reading for the night. It was something for the children and a way to get people together. But I sure was curious about where this massive personality of Girlie's came from. It was like someone flipped a switch, and she became a star in a show when she was up in front of those children tonight. It was too late to ask now, but I'd be sure to ask her the next time I saw her.

THE NEXT MORNING

I was at the coffee shop early to open and was chatting with Edward before we unlocked the door. The coffee was brewing and the danish were all set up. It smelled so good first thing in the morning. Edward started talking about how wonderful it had been to have me back this summer. From the first day we worked together and I stood up to him about the small group of homeless out back coming in to use the rest room, he said he knew I would find a way to make my own way in the shop.

"You've really done great things with the Sunday Story Hour," he said. I was thrilled to have him appreciate it and even more so to have him tell me.

As we unlocked the door for the customers to come in, I saw Martin approaching. I hadn't seen him for a few weeks and hoped everything was okay. As I poured his coffee for him, he told me about an early morning meeting he had and how he had recently gotten a small bonus check for making his quota in opening new accounts with the bank. "It's small stuff compared to what I used to make and do, but honestly, it's so much more gratifying. Between that and helping with the three girls, I feel I am where I am supposed to be in life right now," he said.

"Helping with the three girls?" I didn't realize he was so involved, I thought seeing them at the Fourth of July picnic was just that, a day out that he enjoyed with them. He stirred sugar into his coffee, took a sip, and shook his head no and began to explain: Ariel, Lexi, and Vanessa had been living at the home where Girlie lived. They lived with their mom, but she had relapsed and started shooting heroin. At that time, she had been technically missing for three days. Girlie had taken to sleeping at their apartment each night to help them.

"I knew you said that back then, but I didn't realize it was still that way?" I was surprised to learn this.

"Oh, yes, when they found the girl's mom, she was a mess, and the courts stepped in and took custody away from her. The girls have not seen her except for a few supervised visits since then. Their mom was removed from the house, and unless someone stepped in to take them, they would have gone to foster homes. Girlie and her big heart couldn't let that happen, so she asked if she could move in and be their guardian. Been that way for a few weeks now," Martin sipped his coffee and eyed a muffin in the glass case. I reached in, took the muffin out and handed it to him.

"I had no idea! She never said one word at Sunday Story Hour!" Wow, this news was something!

Martin looked at his watch and said he had to go but told me a bit more about the situation before he did. Girlie had offered to take care of them until their mom was healthy enough to come home and take care of them. Martin would go over at night and have dinner with them a few times a week and help. Although Girlie loved her role, he said it was very tiring at her age to work full-time and have three young girls to take care of. I pictured them all around the dinner table, a happy family and what Martin had dreamed of all his life. Not quite the way he dreamed it but surely worth waiting for.

"No wonder Vanessa said she would be home in time for her bedtime hug!" I exclaimed.

"I've grown quite fond of them, Josie, I have to tell you," he said wistfully. "They needed to be a family. I wanted to be a father, maybe a grandfather, one day, and somehow we all found each other. It's like it was meant to be."

I couldn't help but think again: Common Ground.

It always seemed to find a way, didn't it?

My last week of summer was quickly approaching, and I was excited for my last Sunday Story Hour. It was a bittersweet time. I was excited because we had something special planned, but sort of feeling let down because it was all coming to an end. Either way, school was right around the corner, and if I was ever going to make it in this business on my own, I had to learn the business end of it. And although I had been having fun being home and working all summer, I really missed my roommates and the routine of our campus. I had seen them only twice during the summer. We would have many late nights up, telling stories of our summer I was sure!

Campus life awaited me.

But first, the finale to Summer Story Hour the last Sunday of August!

Brad had agreed to be the reader that week, and he had books about the constellations, the planets, the moon, and the Milky Way. He had books about black holes and life on Mars. I had no idea how he would work it all in, but he said he had a plan to get the kids to the moon and back before the night was through.

I couldn't wait. I already knew I was over the moon for him.

The Final Sunday Story Hour

Brad arrived at the store in the early afternoon to set up for the final story hour. He asked if he could specifically use the far back corner, the corner farthest from the front door and windows. As I was serving and cleaning up, he was busy hopping up and down, on and off a ladder, hanging various things from the ceiling in the coffee shop. After he was done with that, he cleared all the tables away and started building a fire pit in the center of the cleared area. Around the fire pit, he spread blankets and even had a few wooden pieces that looked like tree stumps and rocks. I was mesmerized, watching him, wondering what he was doing. He had promised the finale to Sunday Story Hour would be unforgettable, but I had no idea what his intentions were.

Finally, it was time to close the coffee shop and prepare for the children to arrive. We had planned a special treat at Brad's request of s'mores, so I began laying the ingredients out on a long table near the back of the shop. Brad took out his guitar, some books, and a flashlight and set them beside the biggest rock. When it was time for Story Hour, he greeted everyone at the front door and asked each one of them if they had ever looked up and seen the night sky. They all said yes, of course they had. Everyone agreed it was always very dark unless there was a full moon.

"Are you sure about that? Is it totally dark?" All their heads bobbed up and down, yes it was always dark.

"Then come with me," Brad said and led them to the far back corner of the coffee shop. We had turned off the lights, and even though it was summer and the sun still shining outside, in this far back corner it was quite dark. Brad used his flashlight to lead everyone safely to the back and find a seat on a blanket. The bigger children he directed to the tree stumps and rocks to sit on. He then turned on a special light he had set up that was directed at the ceiling and said, "Are you *sure* we are in total darkness?"

The ceiling twinkled with what looked like thousands of stars. There were streaks along it for the Milky Way and even a few planets. And of course, a big, full, yellow moon lit up the sky.

It was magical.

Brad told the children he was going to read, but the best way to appreciate the beautiful night sky was to lie on your back and just look up. Every child in the room followed his directions, and *ooohs* and *aaaahs* were heard coming from each of them.

I have no idea how he did it, but his light that illuminated the sky suddenly made shooting stars appear and the children clapped and yelled, "I see a shooting star! I see one too!"

Brad began to read a book about the moon, the stars, the Milky Way, and the constellations. The children all lay perfectly still, listening in the dark at the sights they saw in the night sky. When he was done reading the book, he told the children his favorite way to enjoy the night sky had been when he went camping. Always after dinner, they would build a big fire and lie around just gazing at the night sky. He leaned down and "lit" the fire in the fire pit. It was a pretend fire, but it gave the illusion of a real camp fire. He then picked up his guitar and sang a few silly songs about the sun, moon, and stars. They ended with a sing-along of "Twinkle, Twinkle, Little Star."

All I could think was: is it any wonder why I am over the moon for this guy?

After the song ended, we built s'mores to eat. We couldn't toast the marshmallows inside, but the children didn't seem to mind microwaved marshmallows! Sticky with chocolate and marshmallow, they all sat around the table, talking about how many shooting stars they had seen tonight and asking if the moon was really made of cheese. Brad answered all their questions and seemed to thoroughly enjoy every moment.

It was truly a magical night. And what a wonderful way to end the Summer Story Hour at the coffee shop.

"Josie, you have surely outdone yourself this summer. I want to thank you for bringing this idea to my attention and bringing the community a little closer through this. It's not always easy for us to see who our customers are and what they may like other than what the corporate designs are. This has truly been eye-opening to me, and I have been bringing your ideas to some meetings. And although we can't make it happen in each of our shops, I want you to know you are more than welcome to bring this idea back next summer when you return," Mr. Desmond said as we cleaned up after the families had all gone. I hadn't seen him come in and was surprised to hear him call my name.

"Oh, well, thank you," I said, feeling a bit embarrassed. I was happy he was planning for me to come back next summer, but I honestly had not thought that far ahead. I was thrilled he was pleased enough to think of that!

As we closed and locked the shop, I turned to Brad and said, "Is there *nothing* you can't do?" hugging him tight.

"Oh, it wasn't that big of a deal. It's fun. I love the kid's reactions, and I love this sort of thing," he said.

Like I said, I was over the moon for this guy, no doubt about that.

September

Back on campus and in a new dorm but with the same roommates, it was like we had never left. Right back into the routine and right back into the craziness of the schedules.

We spent the first few nights at "welcome back" activities and staying up late to giggle and share our stories about our summers.

We all still wanted to do our volunteer work at Round the Table and agreed we would find time to fit that in. The first week of school was fairly relaxed, so we made a visit by the end of the first week. Everyone there was glad to see us back, and we were happy to see some of the same faces and also some new faces.

Our daily runs along the waterfront before the cold weather would set in were always our favorite part of the day. It was such a release to just get out there and run, feel the wind in your face, fill your lungs and pound your feet to get some energy back after sitting all day in lecture halls.

Life on campus was great, although I missed home and Brad.

It bothered me that I would not be able to keep in close touch with Martin and Girlie and find out how the situation with Ariel, Lexi, and Vanessa was. Girlie remained living with them in their apartment while their mother was away, getting the help she needed. As it was, Girlie had been appointed their legal guardian and had assumed all responsibility for them. Now that summer was over and school was back in session, I was sure it was even harder for her to keep up with all the things they needed while working. I decided I would try to get home more often than I did last year and try to visit. I hoped Martin was able to still be a part of it; he seemed so at ease and natural playing the part of father to them. He had waited all his life to have this role. My heart was happy for him.

Thinking about all the things I had to do, and wanted to do, I was worried I would spread myself too thin and maybe lose some of the fun of what I was doing. I wished Brad lived closer, so I could have him around to talk to. I wished I could visit my Nana and Grandpa more often. Nana, especially, always seemed to have just the perfect advice for me. I almost wished time could speed up and I could be done with school and starting my own life, my own business and my own path in life.

September quickly turned into October, and the cold weather began to whisper its way into the nights and the early mornings. On our runs and on our way to Round the Table, we had seen my veteran friend. I was surprised to see him having dinner at Round the Table one night when we were there.

"College Girl!" he waved when he saw me. "This must be your second year at school? How's the world treating you?" he asked with a big smile.

"Oh, not too shabby," I smiled back. He asked about my summer, and I told him about what I had done with Sunday Story Hour at the coffee shop and how excited I was that it was such a success.

"I knew the minute I met you that you had a heart of gold there." He poked his own chest. "You've just got something in your eyes that looks deeper than most. You really *see* people, and you really *feel* what they are going through. So what do you think you'll do once school is over for you?"

I told him a bit about my plans for my own coffee shop and what I thought it would look like.

"I guess I'll just live by my favorite motto and keep it simple, you know?" I said sort of distracted, thinking about how I had such a dream, but as time went on, I really had no idea how I could ever bring it to become reality.

"Well, what's your motto?" he asked peering up over the menu, trying to decide what to have to eat.

"Live simply, so others may simply live," I said proudly.

"College Girl, I really believe you've got it in you. I'd say nothin' suits you better than that way of thinkin,' and you'll find a way. By the grace of God, if it's meant to be."

"So, what's it gonna be for dinner tonight?" I smiled and pulled out my notepad to write his order down.

November

Midterms were in full swing. We stayed up far too late cramming for the tests and writing papers. None of us had any time in the past two weeks to volunteer, nor for our runs or nearly anything fun. It was crunch time, and it was hitting hard. I hadn't even spoken to Brad in several days. He was busy at school too.

I was in bed reading one night when my phone rang. I glanced at the screen: Call from Mom, it said. I swiped right to answer, "Hey, Mom! Not a good time, can I call you tomorrow?"

There was silence.

"Mom? Can I call you tomorrow?" I asked again.

"Sure, sure. I guess." I could hear the anxiety in my mom's voice. I closed my book and sat up.

"Okay, Mom, what's up?"

"Well, I just wanted to tell you . . ." Her voice trailed off, and I could hear the wavering in it. "I just wanted to tell you . . . Nana is in the hospital. She had a slight stroke. But, honey, don't you worry. I just didn't want you to come home for Thanksgiving and find out. She's doing okay, but she's got a bit of struggle ahead."

"Oh, Mom! No. How bad? Can she talk? Is she paralyzed? Does she know you? Is she going to live? Oh, Mom, I have so many questions! Go ahead, I'll just listen."

She told me Nana was going to be okay and that they were keeping her for a few days just to monitor her. But they felt she was going to be okay. She had slight paralysis in her left hand and leg, but it should resume with therapy. Her speech had not been affected, and she knew everyone. She was already complaining she just wanted to go home.

I asked how it happened. She told me they had been shopping, and Nana felt a bit dizzy, so they went home. After they got home, she felt very sick and couldn't walk straight, so Grandpa had called Mom and then the ambulance. Thankfully they got right to the hospital, or she could have been in much worse shape. Mom said the doctors seemed very confident that she was going to be okay, but would not be home for Thanksgiving.

"You're not just saying that because you don't want me to worry, right?" I asked, tears running down my face.

"Honey, I would not call you and tell you something that would make your last week of school worse, trust me. I just wanted you to know so when you get home you aren't more upset that I didn't tell you. I promise, the doctors are confident," my mom said.

"Can I call and talk to Nana?" I choked out.

"Why don't we call you tomorrow when I am there? It's hard for her to reach the phone, and she can't get out of bed to get it."

I interrupted with a shriek, "She can't get out of bed!"

"Honey, calm down. Yes, she can get out of bed. She's been up walking, but with the slight paralysis on one side, they don't want her up and about by herself. And if she hears the phone, she may try to answer it. So just let me call you when I am there, okay?" my mom tried to soothe my fears.

"Okay, okay." I blew my nose.

I'd be waiting for the call tomorrow. I doubted I would sleep much tonight anyway.

Thanksgiving Break

Midterms done, and packing up for the next few days at home, I realized this was going to be a very different Thanksgiving than how I spent it last year. Instead of working at the coffee shop, having Nana and Grandpa over for turkey and fixin's and then spending that wonderful night at the cabin with my little group of misfit friends, we would spend every day, all day at the rehab center, visiting Nana. She was doing well enough to be released from the hospital within a week of having the stroke, but her progress at rehab was slow. She still had some weakness in her leg and foot and was having trouble with balance. She had fallen just days after arriving, and it set her back a bit in her therapy.

It was great to see her, though. I got home from campus Wednesday night due to my class schedule, and Mom was cooking what she could the night before to be ready for Thursday. We planned to get as much done tonight as we could, get up early and start the turkey so it would be ready for lunchtime. That way, we could visit Nana most of the day. They were having a special dinner for the patients, but she flatly refused to eat their food on Thanksgiving. So we got everything ready, then watched some holiday specials together and were all in bed early.

Thanksgiving Day

I was a little nervous about seeing Nana the first time. She was always such a vibrant and energetic woman. I was afraid to see her in a hospital situation. I wasn't sure she would enjoy me being there either. I knew her too well to think she would not want everyone sitting around, worrying about her. We entered the facility, and it looked so much like a hospital I couldn't stand it. I immediately got nervous and could feel myself starting to sweat. But I had to remain strong and put on a brave face for Nana. We had all the food with us; frankly I thought we brought far too much food.

"Mom, it's just Nana and us, why do we need all this food?" I kept asking as she spooned vegetables, potatoes, stuffing and gravy into bowls to travel. Dad was slicing the turkey and piling it on a large platter to bring with us.

"It's *Thanksgiving*, honey! We want to have enough to share in case Nana has made some friends who will want to join us for dinner."

I rolled my eyes and laughed.

"Sure, Mom, Nana's been there all of a couple of weeks and made tons of friends, you think?"

"You never know. You know your grandmother." She smiled back.

As we turned the corner to the hall where they said Nana's room was, I saw a room in the corner all decorated for a nice dinner. Mom took the food in there and said, "We'll just set this all here and go get her."

We turned back down the hall to her room. As we got closer, we were greeted by Nana making her way slowly down the hall with her walker! I almost shouted for joy but clasped my hand over my mouth to prevent it. I didn't want to frighten her and cause her to fall again. We just stopped and watched silently as she took one step with her walker, two steps with her walker and inched her way closer to us. Her head bent to watch her feet; I could see her mouth, "One foot forward, move the walker. Next foot forward."

Slowly, slowly she made her way. And she looked fantastic! Dressed for dinner, her hair and lipstick flawless, her shoes on, and a sweater around her shoulders. It probably took her all morning to primp and be ready for this holiday debut! I held back my tears and held my breath waiting for her to notice we were there.

Just then, she looked up to see how far she had left to travel down the hall. Her face lit up when she saw us, and she moved a bit faster.

"Happy Thanksgiving!" She beamed at all of us.

"Nana! You look *amazing!*" I reached around the walker to hug her.

"Well, yes, I do, if I do say so myself," she said.

Grandpa leaned over to kiss her and pat her on the hand. This must have been tough for him being alone these past few weeks.

"How's my lady?" he asked her.

"Hungry!" she said.

We made our way slowly back to the room in the corner. As we got close, I could hear voices coming from the room. *Oh dear*, I thought. *We won't be alone in there. It must be a common dining room for families on holidays.* My heart sank a bit. I had selfishly wanted Nana all to myself today at least.

We turned the corner into the room, and I couldn't believe it! Sitting at the table was Brad, Martin, Girlie, Green Leaf, Bonkers, Ariel, Lexi, and Vanessa!

"Happy Thanksgiving!" they all said in unison! They had set the table and had all the food arranged on another table next to them. It smelled delicious.

"We did Thanksgiving for you last year, it's your turn to host us," Green Leaf said and everyone laughed.

Martin got up and pulled out a chair at the head of the table. "For the lady," he said and helped Nana into the chair. Next to her, he helped Grandpa get settled. Oh my goodness. How selfish was I wanting her all to myself? She deserved this wonderful party!

We stayed there all day and into the evening. We ate so much our tummies hurt. We laughed so much our tummies hurt. And just when we thought we couldn't eat another bite, Green Leaf brought out several pies he had made. We had pecan, apple, pumpkin, and blueberry.

"This guy's got some great talent in the kitchen, I tell ya," Bonkers said. We all agreed by nodding, our mouths full of pie.

Everyone took turns telling stories about what they had been doing, how school was, how therapy was, how work was and, of course, we all took turns saying what we were thankful for.

Vanessa had asked if she could start the blessing, which of course, we all said we thought that was only fitting.

"This year, I am thankful for people who have taken us in when we needed it the most. Although Mom is not here, I am thankful she is still getting what she needs to be healthy. I am thankful for the chance to stay in school, in my own house, and with my sisters."

She got a mumbled "amen" all around the table.

Girlie smiled at her and nodded. A proud mother-daughter moment almost.

Green Leaf said he was thankful for the chance to still be cooking at the shop and to have a warm place to live. Bonkers was thankful for the chance to teach art after school to the children at the youth center. He said he wished it paid a bit more, but living with Green Leaf, he was thankful for the chance to just do art again.

Martin was thankful for so many blessings he said. Maybe too many to count, but mostly he was thankful for having a family he could be a part of. I saw him wink at Girlie when he was done, and she smiled back at him. It was then I noticed: She had her new teeth!

Girlie said she was thankful for being part of a family as well, but mostly for the blessings of the love and wisdom of the children given to her to nurture. She said it made her feel *whole* and loved. She was thankful to receive love.

Lexi and Ariel echoed their sister. Too young to really form their thoughts, they just said "We are thankful for all of you and thankful our mom is getting better."

Mom, Dad, and Grandpa were thankful for Nana's progress and the doctors who helped her and for the time to spend with me on this brief visit home.

Nana said she was just thankful to have another Thanksgiving with all of us on this side of the dirt! Typical Nana, always making light of a serious situation, but her humor was what got her to this ripe, old age, I suppose.

Brad was thankful for all the opportunities given to him at school, at work, and for having me in his life. We didn't talk every day, but he said he was thankful I was in his heart and always there in spirit.

I went last and had the hardest time. My heart was so full; it was hard to put into words what I felt at that moment. I was thankful for such wonderful family, friends, and the many blessings I had witnessed with just this small group gathered around this table.

Round the Table. Common Ground.

Somehow it kept coming back to these things.

So many good things had come into my life, I was truly blessed.

We raised our glasses and toasted with apple cider.

"To another year of blessings!"

I learned that afternoon that the girls' mother had made wonderful progress and was now allowed to leave the facility where she was required to stay. She could come for visits to the apartment and had been looking to start a job soon. She would need to stay at the facility when she began the job as part of her recovery process. Oftentimes, the stress of leaving, going to work, and resuming some responsibility proved too great and the answer was to return to drugs. If she stayed near the facility and had her check-ins and stayed clean, she should be home within a few months. I was happy for them, but worried what would become of Girlie after all this time of having them in her life.

And I asked Girlie about her new teeth!

"Well, that is a vibrant smile you have there!" I said as we cleaned up the dishes.

"Oh, I know! I look like a movie star, don't you think?" And she flashed me a big fake smile.

"I think you look very natural, very happy, and very beautiful." I couldn't believe how happy she looked. It came from inside; she had waited all her life to be a mom, and this surely agreed with her. I was so happy for her.

Mid-December

My first semester of my second year of college had gone so fast, and I was pleased with my grades. I had been able to keep up my volunteer times at Round the Table and also keep a fairly good social life on campus. My roommates and friends always had meals together, often cooking and having study nights together.

As the cold wind began to whisper along the river, our days of running outside became forgotten, and instead, we ran inside on the track or just went to work out in the gym. It always felt better to run outside and let the wind and the pounding of my feet bring my stress level down, but a good workout, time with friends, and some good food always did the trick too.

With the first snowfall, I packed my belongings in the car and drove home for another Christmas and winter break. I planned to work at the coffee shop, but I also planned to spend one day a week with my grandparents. Nana was doing great, but they needed some help with a few things. And I felt it would be good for me to visit them. Since she still had some things to overcome, they would not be going to Florida as early as they had last year. If they were still going to be there when my spring break came, I planned to visit for a few days then. The timetable all depended on how Nana did recovering. I was nervous about the winter and her getting around.

Christmas break began as a gentle snow began to fall, and we awoke the next morning to nearly six inches of snow on the ground. It snowed every day for the next week! It was the first time in a very long time we would have a white Christmas. And it was bone-chilling cold. Shoppers in the downtown area were coming to the coffee shop for coffee and hot chocolate in bunches. My shifts there went by so quickly I barely had time to think!

Part of me was glad I didn't have time to think. I missed Brad, and I missed my friends. I missed my times out back getting to know Martin and Girlie and seeing how their lives were shaping up. I would see Martin when he stopped in for coffee, but now it was like he was just a regular customer. Girlie would stop in, too, but usually after school with the girls she was still taking care of. One day, their mom was with them, and I had a chance to meet her and talk with her. She was so humble and grateful for all Girlie had done for her and thanked me for helping to take care of Girlie when she was alone.

"It really is true. There are some really nice folks out there. I didn't see it before. I was too young and stupid and hooked on those darn drugs to realize. I thank God every day my girls are as smart as they are and realizing how important it is to be nice and just help others. I'm doing really well with my treatments, and I hope to be working full-time soon and able to move back home."

I was happy to see she was committed to not just her girls, but also to her recovery. I could feel she meant what she said. It seemed by late spring, she could be back in her own apartment.

I wondered what would happen to Girlie when that day came.

Spring Break

Time seemed to be going so fast. I was on my way to Florida to visit Nana and Grandpa and also Brad. He had decided to change his time and go while I was there as well this year. We had such a good time; he wanted to visit again and spend the time together. He would not be bringing Harvey this time, though. He said last year, he had driven, and Harvey was his copilot. This year, being a shorter visit, he decided to fly, and it would just be too much to try and get Harvey there. We would all miss Harvey.

Nana was doing great. Her limp was barely noticeable, and her memory had not been affected at all from the stroke. She walked every day in the warm Florida weather and loved sitting on the beach or on her deck having lunch or lemonade in the warm Florida breezes. Brad and I didn't do much except relax. At home, I had worked the first four days of break and was spending the last five days here, so it was nice to just lie around, walk on the beach, drink lemonade, play games and have lunch or dinner with all the retired folks.

It seemed funny to me to think in just two short years, I would be starting my life, my career, and my real adult years. All the folks here were done with all that and enjoying their retirements. Two opposite ends of life, yet we had found something in common: the beach!

The ultimate common ground!

Two Years Later

I could hardly believe it; the four years of college were winding down, and I was setting my sights on graduation and what I would do with my life. The only sure thing I had was that I knew Brad would always be a part of it.

As I wrapped up the first semester of my senior year, I had much to think about. I had been doing more time at Round the Table to learn a bit more about how it ran as I knew I wanted to have a non-profit business myself when I graduated. I still had that $10,000 I had won on the lottery ticket Nana and Grandpa gave me, and I had banked several thousand dollars of my own money by being very frugal working at the coffee shop. But still, in order to run a nonprofit, I had to have some sort of backing and monetary support. I needed to learn this. Or I needed a rich fairy to just plop down in front of me and say, "Here you go!" I was literally banking on the first option, but how?

One night, as I was working at Round the Table, I noticed Mr. Desmond standing in line outside. He was in line like all the others, waiting for a table. Curious, I walked closer to the window, so he would see me inside. He waved and nodded. Mr. Desmond was the area boss of the coffee shop where I worked back home, whatever would he be doing in the city coming to dinner at a co-op community kitchen?

I saw him speaking with the host and then walked to one of the tables I was serving. When he was seated, I walked over and said, "Good evening. Welcome to Round the Table. Is this your first time here?"

"Yes, it is. And may I comment, it is far more beautiful than I ever imagined," he said, his eyes sweeping around the room. He told me having heard me talk about it so often, he felt he needed to come see it.

We chatted a bit about the menu, and a few more guests were seated with him. Before long, they were all chatting and eating their salads.

As I refilled his water glass, I noticed him look up at a table, and his face drained of color. He wiped his mouth with his napkin and drank some water. He returned to eating his salad, but he never rejoined the conversation around the table. He kept his eyes forward. As I walked away, I gazed over to see who or what he seemed so interested in, or more importantly, why it seemed to startle him so much.

My gaze moved to the table by the window where my veteran friend sat. He had become quite a regular there, even worked a few shifts washing dishes. He would sing in his alto voice in the kitchen, and it would carry out to the dining area, thrilling the guests. He even meandered around the dining area a few times, serenading a few for special occasions. Or no occasion, just because it made everyone smile. His voice and smile were contagious, for sure!

I saw him eating his spaghetti and engaged in an animated conversation with the others at his table. No surprise there and nothing out of the ordinary.

I gazed back at Mr. Desmond. The color had returned to his face, but his entrée sat in front of him, untouched. He watched the veteran and drank his water. I moved to refill it, and he grabbed my arm, "Josie, do you know that man over there? The man by the window with one arm and one leg? I mean, do you *know* him?" his voice croaked, barely a whisper, and I detected a vague shaking in his voice.

"No, sir, I don't," I answered back.

"Do you know *anything* about him?" he asked, tightening his grip on my arm. I could feel his fingers shaking through my sleeve.

"I know he is a veteran, has a great voice, and is one of the happiest people I have ever met." But I could offer no more. I thought someone had said his name was George one time, but I really wasn't sure. I was embarrassed to think, in all this time, I had never asked his name.

"I think his name might be George," I said as I looked over at him.

Mr. Desmond pushed his plate away and stood. Tears were running down his cheeks.

"I . . . I . . . I . . . have to find a reason to speak with him," he said, wiping his face.

"Um, okay, sir. Maybe I could . . ." And Mr. Desmond got up and walked over to the other man's table, sat across from him, and shook his hand. I saw the veteran look shocked, push his chair back, and just stare at Mr. Desmond for what seemed an eternity. His throat bobbed as he swallowed, and he wiped his own face, not from tears but from sweat that had suddenly broken out on his face. I didn't know what to do, so I stood, mute, just watching the scene.

Mr. Desmond reached across the table and shook his hand. I heard the veteran say, "Yes, I am, I am George," and Mr. Desmond got up and hugged him.

George and Mr. Desmond stayed in the hug for what seemed forever, and then both men leaned back, looked into each other faces, and embraced again. I could hear Mr. Desmond sobbing.

I realized this was a very private moment, albeit very public, and I was eavesdropping. I began to circulate and check on my customers, cleaning tables, filling water glasses, bringing dessert.

"Josie, Josie, please, come meet my uncle!" I heard as I came out of the kitchen.

"This is my uncle Ernest!" the veteran said, his arm around Mr. Desmond's shoulder.

"And *this* is my *nephew*, George!" Mr. Desmond beamed; his arm around the veteran's shoulder.

"Oh! Oh my goodness!" I clasped my hand over my mouth.

And that began a very long story from the two of them about how George had been sent on duty and had gone missing for several months. He had become a prisoner of war. His family had not been able to locate him, and when he was found, he was diagnosed with amnesia as well as the two missing limbs. He spent several months in a hospital on an Army base in Germany. When he had been found, he had no dog tags or other form of identification on him. It took several months to identify him, and his family thought he had been killed. They waited months for him to come home. George had been released from the hospital and put together a life without knowing who he really was.

"That must be a very hard life to live," I said with tears in my eyes. "Did you have *any* idea who you really were or that they were looking for you?"

"It came back to me in snippets; I eventually knew my name and had flashes of my life. I think that's how I got here, I knew I was from this area, and I stayed with other vets at shelters, and it just sort of became normal for me. I was like a gypsy, a nomad—a man without a home. I got by. By the time I remembered enough to know who I was, well, I've just been too embarrassed to try and get back to my life. I'm proud of who I was, what I did, and how I served our country, but I'm not proud of what I have become.

"I just have a tough time taking all this in, you know? I never thought I'd see my family again. I knew I was from this area, I know I belong here, but I don't feel like I really belong anywhere anymore. I like to stay under the radar, as the saying goes," George said, still with that smile on his face.

"So, where will you be staying tonight?" Mr. Desmond asked George.

"Oh, I got a room over at the men's shelter on Oak Street," George perked up.

Mr. Desmond looked anxious. I knew he wanted to jump in and just fix it all, but this wasn't something you could just fix. I had learned from seeing so many homeless, down on their luck and addicted individuals that although the situation wasn't ideal and it was of course where nobody would choose to be, part of most of their make up in their personality was to *own* who they were. I guess it was sort of a survival of the fittest.

George said he had to get going to the men's shelter. If he wasn't in by 8:00 p.m., they locked the doors, and he would be out on the streets for the night. He had a room; it was his room for as long as he needed it, but he had to live by the rules.

"When will I see you again? How can I reach you?" Mr. Desmond asked.

"How about you come by tomorrow, and we can talk a bit? I don't want anyone to know I'm here yet, okay? I need time to think about this. I'm still fuzzy on some of my past, and I can't let myself get overwhelmed. It's not been easy, you know?" George's eyes pleaded with Mr. Desmond although his voice remained strong.

"Of course, I'll respect your wishes," Mr. Desmond said and watched George walk out the door.

I let out a breath; I hadn't realized I had been holding it. I closed my eyes and said a quick prayer.

Graduation Day

Here we all stood. All pomp and circumstance. Our gowns shining in the sun. Our caps askew as nobody really knew how it was truly supposed to fit on our head. Tassels on the appropriate side. Lined up like soldiers. Last minute hugs. Smiles and tears.

Families standing to see us as we entered under the tent. Cameras flashing. The music playing, the flags of our schools leading us down the aisle. I saw my parents, Nana, and Grandpa with Brad, cameras all up, smiles across their faces. I smiled and waved.

"*Yeah*, Josie!" I heard the shout from my left. Lined up outside the tent was a crowd of people who may not have a ticket but wanted to see the ceremony.

"*Jooosieee!*" I heard it again, and then I realized it was Bonkers yelling! I saw him in the crowd, jumping up and down, yelling my name. He was surrounded by Green Leaf, Girlie, and Martin! They were all waving and jumping like kids. I smiled and waved.

I couldn't believe they were here to see me graduate!

The ceremony was glorious. I wanted to enjoy every minute of it. There were serious moments, lighthearted moments and speeches to remember for a lifetime. As names were read and the graduates accepted their degrees, the crowd cheered for each name. Somehow, it seemed my name got the loudest cheer with my group of misfits just outside the tent going nuts over me. I felt like a celebrity.

We posed for pictures after. First with friends and family, then a few candid shots that my dad took as we mingled in the crowd. After a while, Bonkers, Green Leaf, Girlie, and Martin made their way through the crowd and hugged me like I was never going to see them again.

"So proud of you!" Martin beamed.

"Well, don't you all look extra nice today?" I said, looking at all of them dressed up and looking wonderful!

It was then that I noticed, each of them had a lollipop sticking out of their jacket pocket. Girlie's was pinned to her shirt just above her heart.

Martin noticed I was looking at their lollipops and said, "We wanted him to be here with us. He was so proud of you, Josie. It's our way of keeping him here and close to our hearts. We have one for you. You can wear to your party later." And Girlie pinned it on my graduation gown.

Fighting back tears, I held the lollipop between my fingers and smiled. "He is here for sure."

I saw my parents and grandparents watching us. They knew how special these folks had become to me. It was hard to believe four years ago, they were living on the streets, and now, they all had jobs and places of their own to live. We'd been on this journey together for four years, and somehow I felt it was just beginning in so many ways.

We took one last photo then: Martin stood next to Girlie, Green Leaf next to Bonkers, Brad and me in the front, with our arms around each other we stuck our lollipops in our mouths and yelled, "Cheers!"

A Month after Graduation

I had returned home and stayed working at the coffee shop while I spent time deciding how to get my coffee shop going. I was looking at places to rent, and everything in our town was out of my price range. I felt like I needed to be in the city where I had gone to school and where I saw the greatest need. The folks at Round the Table were being amazingly helpful in getting me connections and giving me ideas to get my business going. My dream of working with Samantha and Kelsie had sort of been put away as Samantha found a job before school ended. She took a job at the major hotel chain where she interned and was currently living in another city to open a new branch of the chain. She planned to return within the year and be based in our city, but until then, I had to go get used to not seeing her every day like I had for the past four years.

Kelsie had also returned home while she looked for a job. As a restaurant manager, she had lots of opportunities, but she wanted to find just the right one and not jump at just any opportunity. She lived about forty-five minutes away from me, so we got together during the week if we could to have dinner or shop and just try to capture some of the fun we used to have in the city.

I missed all of us being together.

I tried to get to Round the Table as often as I could, but now that I had to drive into the city, it was tough to work a full shift after I had been at work all day. I loved going in to meet with everyone and suggested to Kelsie that we meet there for dinner one night instead of going to another place.

"It will be like old times," I said and she agreed.

"I couldn't agree more, I miss those times for sure!"

As I was leaving work, I noticed a flyer had been put up in the office, announcing Mr. Desmond's retirement. He hardly seemed old enough to retire! I quickly jotted the date of his retirement party in my calendar and left to meet Kelsie at Round the Table for dinner.

Mr. Desmond's Retirement Party

We all gathered at a restaurant near our home office for Mr. Desmond's retirement party. It was fun to see my coworkers outside of work casually and even more fun to have a chance to see Ms. Gaines outside of work. There were several people of upper management and lots of people from some of the other shops he had overseen as the area boss.

Cocktails and easy conversation to open the evening were fun and such a great ice breaker with this mix of people. As I chatted with a few people I casually knew from the shop, Mr. Desmond caught my eye in the crowd and motioned for me to come over. I excused myself and made my way across the room.

"Well, happy retirement, Mr. Desmond!" I grinned. I knew this was a happy occasion for him, but in the back of my mind, I was rather sad. I had grown to respect and appreciate him as a big boss, and more importantly, I had seen the human, compassionate side of him when he found his nephew George. I had seen George a few times at Round the Table and knew Uncle Ernest had brought him back together with much of his family and that he got George out of the shelter and living in a group home for veterans who needed some medical, psychological, and financial help. He didn't live as close to Round the Table now, so he wasn't a frequent customer. But he still continued to come and work a few shifts when he was able to.

"Thank you, yes it's time." Mr. Desmond sighed. He said he was retiring a bit early since he had recently been diagnosed with cancer and wanted time to enjoy life. He said he had made more than enough money to live comfortably for a few years, and while he was going to be undergoing chemo treatments, he would not be working. So retirement seemed the best solution.

"Oh, I'm so sorry, I hadn't heard," I said.

"Well, after finding George and realizing how much time we had lost with him, I started to re-evaluate my life anyway. I realized I had been working and working and making money and never really had time to enjoy it. I never had time to live the life I wanted. And I want you to know, Josie, a lot of what you said has stuck in my mind."

I was flattered, but honestly, could my outlook on life really be an influence on a man like him?

"And that is what I want to talk with you about. I have a lot of money invested in the company, and when I retire, I will be taking a large portion and donating it to a worthy cause," he said very seriously.

"That is a very noble gesture, Mr. Desmond, I'm sure you will make whatever organization or cause you choose very pleased," I smiled.

"Josie, I want to donate to *your* cause. I want to be the financial backing to your coffee shop." He smiled back.

I took a deep breath in and let it blow out. I couldn't believe what I was hearing. I had been searching for a way to make it happen, and here it was. Could I accept his offer?

How could I not?

"And I hope you will respond because it looks like they are about to start with the formalities, and I want to present my retirement plans publicly here tonight." He winked.

"Ah, sure, no pressure?" I laughed.

"Just say yes," he pleaded with his eyes.

"Yes! Of course, yes! And thank you!"

I wanted to find someone in the crowd to pinch me. Could this really be happening? I had dreamed of this for so long, could it really be happening now?

The Beginning of Common Ground

Mr. Desmond had said he wanted to name the coffee shop Josie's, but I quickly said no to that. I didn't feel right about having my name up there above the door. This coffee shop was not going to be about me; it was going to be a place for people to gather, relax, and communicate—a way to escape the everyday pressures.

"Well, I certainly understand that, but why not? It's an honor to have your name on your business," Mr. Desmond playfully argued back.

I explained to him how all through my life since I had started this dream, one idea kept coming back to me. It was how people who never knew each other were able to come together through some sort of common ground: to find a bond. I found it with my roommates that first weekend at school. We all found it at Round the Table. My misfit friends and I found it with just having open hearts and caring for one another. The examples were many.

"I think my shop should be called Common Ground. It's a theme in relationships and a twist on how coffee is made.

And so it was: Common Ground.

Mr. Desmond found a great location in the city near enough to Round the Table that I would be able to have some of the regulars from there as well as college students, people working in the city, and anyone who happened to find us.

We designed our menu like Round the Table and decided a cup of coffee would be $2. I only had one size, what would be considered medium at a chain coffee shop. I wanted fresh food available, but a simple menu. I brought Green Leaf in to help design the menu and offered him the chance to be my main chef. He designed some fantastic sandwiches on homemade bread and croissants and then went to work designing the gardens for our home grown vegetables and herbs.

While Green Leaf was busy designing the food portion of Common Ground, Bonkers was busy painting several murals on the walls, depicting scenes from local spots and casual coffee connections. People along the waterfront drinking coffee, children at a story hour inside a coffee house, and people working in a garden outside a coffee house picking vegetables. It was all coming together.

"What will your logo be?" Mr. Desmond asked me one day.

I hadn't thought about that. Did I need one? Did I want people to see my coffee cup logo and know where I was and what I was about?

Did I want the message of the nymph with a name written in black underneath it going out into the world?

I didn't think I did.

I think my logo would be simple: a coffee cup tipped over in a saucer, spilling coffee with a puff of steam coming out of it. The steam would take the shape of a heart.

"Sort of like you are spilling the rhetoric of coffee these days?" Mr. Desmond asked.

"Exactly." I winked and smiled.

After we decided on our menu and had the murals designed, we began to work out details of how much everything would cost. Keeping it simple: Sandwiches would be $2. Dessert items would be $2, and salads would be $3. I wanted to do something similar to Round the Table and have the option to pay or come back and work it off, but being a smaller scale operation, that was difficult to figure out. I would not need as many people working since we wouldn't be serving meals. I decided to give it a try and decided the work choices would be: serve at the counter, bus and clean, or work in the gardens. We planned to have greenhouses to provide fresh vegetables year round. Martin and Brad built the greenhouses, supervised by my Grandpa. I also wanted to include the option of talent as a way to work and give back. I wanted to continue the story hour that I had started at home and also thought it might be fun to have an open mic night for local talent. One of the things I enjoyed most about the coffee shop at home was when the local schools would bring the children in for their holiday programs. I wanted that in my shop.

While we were brainstorming ideas for the murals, Bonkers would paint. I shared some of my favorite quotes that I lived by, various philosophical messages, and uplifting ideas I had found along my way in life.

I was surprised and humbled when I entered the shop for our final walk through the day before opening to find Bonkers had made an entire wall of quotes along the back wall.

As you entered the shop, to your right, he had painted the long stretch of wall a gorgeous cream color and, using calligraphy, hand wrote each quote in black. Interspersed between the quotes were photos showing the progress of the shop's construction. The photos were framed in black to compliment the calligraphy.

"Where did these photos come from?" I asked in amazement.

"Girlie has been here nearly every day, taking them," he said, pointing out a few of the highlights.

I hadn't even realized! I knew she was coming by every day to see the progress, but I hadn't realized she was photographing it! What a precious gift that I would treasure and share with all my guests.

"Bonkers, these murals are outstanding. I can't thank you enough. I don't know how you got this done with your jobs at the senior center and youth center!" I hugged him to show my appreciation

"Aw, it was nothing. It gave me something to do at night when I wasn't busy anyway. I love working with the kids after school, and I love teaching the seniors how to paint. But this was my alone time, time to think and create. It's been special. I want to thank you!" He hugged me back.

And then I noticed the tables! Hand cut, carved, and varnished to a high, gleaming polish. I walked closer. Each one was a bit different: shape, color, and texture.

"Where did these come from?" I gasped, running my hand along one.

"Green Leaf's family did some work on the farm and needed to cut some trees down, so we saved them and carved these tables. Green Leaf did the cutting and carving. I did the artwork.

I hadn't even noticed! Each one had a saying etched into the surface.

"Live simply, so others may simply live."

Mahatma Ghandi.

"My religion is very simple. My religion is kindness."

Dalai Lama.

"Be patient. Everything comes to you in the right moment"

Buddha.

I was moving along, looking at all the sayings on the tables. Shaking and crying by the end, I couldn't believe it.

"How did you know? How did you know some of my favorite sayings?" I ran my hand over the smooth shiny tables.

"I may have seen them when you were writing your journal," Brad said.

"Well, I forgive you for snooping!" I leaned over to kiss him.

"There's one more you need to see." He took my hand and led me to the main serving counter.

A long, four-foot counter, again shining brilliantly with all we would need to open in just two days!

A large jar of lollipops sat next to the register.

"A little reminder for all our customers to always see the child in you," Martin said.

And then I noticed: "Serve up quality, and you'll never lack for hearts around your table" was scripted along the front edge of the counter.

"Oh, Nana's saying. I love it. Thank you all so much!"

Then I realized there was a heart crafted at the end of the saying, and in it sat a small box.

"Open it, dear," Nana said.

I opened the box to find a sparkling diamond ring.

"To new beginnings. To life. Will you marry me, Josie?" Brad grinned.

"Yes, yes, a thousand times *yes!*"

"Well, I believe we are now ready for the grand opening of Common Ground!" Martin cheered from behind us.

"To Common Ground! To Josie!" shouted Mr. Desmond and began passing champagne.

The End

About the Author

Other than being a mom, being a published author is the greatest reward I ever imagined. I have written since I was a child and believe stories, books, and writing can take you anywhere you want to be in life. I love gardening, photography and traveling out west.

CPSIA information can be obtained
at www.ICGtesting.com
Printed in the USA
BVHW02s0803010518
514911BV00026B/181/P